FOOTSUCKER

Geoff Nicholson was born in Sheffield and educated at the Universities of Cambridge and Essex. His novels include *Street Sleeper, What We Did on Our Holidays, Hunters and Gatherers, The Errol Flynn Novel, Still Life With Volkswagens* and *Everything and More*. He has also published two works of non-fiction: *Big Noises* and *Day Trips to the Desert*. Geoff Nicholson lives in London.

FOOTSUCKER

Geoff Nicholson

VICTOR GOLLANCZ · LONDON

First published in Great Britain 1995
in hardback and paperback
by Victor Gollancz
An imprint of the Cassell Group
Wellington House, 125 Strand, London WC2R 0BB

A catalogue record for this book is
available from the British Library.

ISBN 0 575 06024 7 hb
ISBN 0 575 06093 X pb

10   9   8   7   6   5   4   3   2

Photoset in Great Britain by
Rowland Phototypesetting Ltd, Bury St Edmunds, Suffolk
Printed and bound in Great Britain by
Mackays of Chatham plc, Chatham, Kent

FOOTSUCKER

I love feet. They talk to me. As I take them in my hands I feel their strengths, their weaknesses, their vitality or their failings. A good foot, its muscles firm, its arch strong, is a delight to touch, a masterpiece of divine workmanship. A bad foot – crooked toes, ugly joints, loose ligaments moving under the skin – is an agony. As I take these feet in my hands I am consumed with anger and compassion: anger that I cannot shoe all the feet in the world, compassion for all those who walk in agony.

Salvatore Ferragamo, *Shoemaker of Dreams*

Just as the fetish enables the fetishist to simultaneously recognize and deny woman's castration, irony allows the ironist to both reject and reappropriate the discourse of reference.

Naomi Schor, 'Fetishism and Its Ironies'
in *Nineteenth Century French Studies*, Fall 1988

One

I held her feet in my hands. They were perfect, of course; as pale and pure and cold as vellum. I kissed them, let my lips move softly and drily over their insteps, then placed them gently on the floor by the bed. I took a final long, lingering look. I wanted always to remember them this way.

Then I took a claw hammer, previously unused, all shiny burnished steel, with a rubber sheath around the handle to give grip and absorb shock. I raised it high above my head, let it balance at the peak of its apex, and then I brought it down as hard and as precisely as I could, down on to the cold, pale, white, left foot. I did it again for the right. Then several times more, again and again, until the feet were no longer perfect, indeed no longer recognizable as feet, until they were smashed, disordered, pulverized, scattered to all points of the room.

White dust hung low in the air. White fragments littered the floor, and I gathered them together, crumbling them between my fingers. Of course there was no blood, no flesh, no splinters of bone, no smashed tissue. All I had done was destroy two plaster casts of Catherine's feet. The real ones were still intact, still perfect, although they were no longer accessible to me.

I had hoped that destroying the casts might act as a kind of therapy, as a kind of voodoo. I had hoped that destroying the replicas might also destroy the hold that Catherine's feet had over me. As I sat on the floor, surrounded by plaster rubble, I knew that the magic hadn't worked. I was as deeply in thrall as ever.

Two

This is what used to happen. This is what I used to do. This is how it usually went. I stood on street corners looking presentable. I wore a good suit with a plain tie. I looked smart and clean and boyish. I had a pen in one hand and a clipboard in the other, and I tried my very hardest to look unthreatening. I tried to be charming and I tried to make my smile sincere. Then I would stop women in the street and ask if they'd be prepared to answer a few simple questions. I often stood close to a shoe shop and approached women as they came out, because I could see they'd either bought shoes or at the very least had been looking at them and trying them on. Shoes and feet were already on these women's minds and that helped a lot.

I would tell them that I was attached to a fashion PR company, doing research on behalf of shoe manufacturers, and would they be prepared to talk to me about the kind of shoes they bought and wore.

Naturally, I didn't stop just anybody. I only stopped women who looked right, who were wearing the right type of shoes. Of course, a certain percentage of women just said no. They were busy, or they were in a hurry, or they weren't interested in shoes, or they didn't like being stopped by a strange man in the street however presentable he looked, or they thought I was trying to sell them something. I always did my best to reassure them that I wasn't a salesman, but some of them just wouldn't be reassured. Nevertheless, a large, perhaps a surprisingly large, number of women were prepared to take the time to answer my questions.

I tried not to be intrusive. I didn't ask for names or ages, occupations or details of income or socio-economic group, nothing like that. The first thing I wanted to know was simply how many pairs of shoes the woman owned, and what kind they were, what they were made of, how many in leather, how many in suede, how high the heels were, whether they were slingbacks or court shoes or strappy sandals, what colours they were, whether any of them came from the great and famous shoe manufacturers.

Assuming all this went well, I would move on to questions about the feet themselves, whether the woman had any problems with her feet, whether she had corns or calluses, bunions or scars or fallen arches or hammer toes. In some cases, depending on the type of shoes the woman was wearing, I could see much of this quite plainly, but it was still good to ask. Then I would enquire whether she'd ever had a foot massage or a professional pedicure, and whether she painted her toenails and if so in what colours.

At this point, rather disingenuously, I would act as though the interview was over. The woman would be surprised. She had thought it would take longer than that. She might even say, 'Is that all?' But then, almost as an afterthought, as though it was a matter of no consequence whatsoever, I would ask was it all right if I took her photograph in the interests of research. The woman would always say no, would turn her head, put up a hand to cover her face, say she hated having her picture taken. I would apologize for any embarrassment and say sorry, no, no, I wouldn't ever presume to take a photograph of her *face*. I just wanted to photograph her feet and shoes. She would be relieved at this and usually said OK. Well, to be honest, not all of them used to say OK. For some this was going too far, was just the wrong side of strange, and they said no, in which case I let them go on their way with no argument. But again, a surprising number of women *would* let a strange man photograph their feet in the middle of a busy London street. Or perhaps they felt safer precisely because the street was busy and the act so public.

I would put down my clipboard and produce a serious, professional-looking camera. I would kneel at the woman's feet, peer through the lens, focus, get a good angle, while all the time making it clear that I wasn't trying to look up her skirt, and then I took as many photographs as I decently could. When I sensed the woman was getting bored or restless, I stood up again, put away the camera and said that the interview had gone very well indeed and that since she had been such a helpful respondent would she be prepared to answer a few supplementary questions, that is if she wanted to, if she didn't mind, if I wasn't delaying her too much.

Assuming she agreed, I would ask whether, in her opinion, women dress for themselves, for other women or for men. Regardless of the answer I then asked whether the man, or men, in the woman's life appreciated the shoes she wore. Did they ever, for example, ask her to wear very high heels? If we had got this far, the answer was invariably yes. I asked her to describe the feeling of wearing high heels. She would say that she felt good, strong, high and mighty, attractive, sexy.

Then I would ask whether she ever kept her shoes on during sex. And if I was given the chance I then asked if her sexual partner ever kissed or licked her toes. Did he

13

like her to massage his cock with her bare feet? Did he ever ask her to run her high heels over his balls and buttocks? Did he ever ejaculate into the cleavage of her toes? And so on.

It was during this phase that the interview would invariably come to an abrupt halt. Some women would simply look at me with contempt and anger and walk away. Some would call me a pathetic wanker, some threatened me with violence, either their own or their husband's or boyfriend's. One woman said she'd like to kick me in the balls but I was probably the kind of pervert who'd enjoy it. (She was quite wrong, incidentally.) And one or two had been known to say they were going to call the police.

Almost all these threats were just that. Retribution never came. I was never hit. The police were never summoned, and if they had been, I would have been long gone by the time they arrived. And even if they had arrived in time, what would they have done? Surely the police in central London have better things to do than arrest presentable young men who are doing nothing more sinister than interviewing women about their feet and footwear. And, equally, surely women have far greater things to fear than somebody like me. I was always, and still am, completely harmless.

So that was it. That's what I used to do. That's all. It was no big deal. On the scale of human depravity and perversity it barely registered. There was no violence, no violation, no pain, no victim. Later I would take the questionnaire, which was a genuine document designed and devised by me, and file it away, along with any photographs I'd taken, which I would have had developed and printed and, in certain cases, blown up. This material became part of my archive. More about the archive (much, much more) later.

Subsequently I would lay out these photographs, pore over them, savour the intricacies of foot and shoe, and if I happened to become aroused by this, and if I used the pictures as an aid to masturbation, well, what harm was there in that?

So that's what I usually did. That's what usually happened. But this was a long time ago, and it's not at all what happened when I met Catherine. With Catherine it went very differently.

It was a hot summer's afternoon, a Friday. I was taking an extended lunch break. My suit was too hot but I didn't want to loosen my tie, and I had positioned myself in South Molton Street in readiness to quiz women as they came out of the expensive clothes and shoe shops there.

You couldn't help noticing Catherine. She looked great. She was very tall, statuesque even, not thin, not girlish. She had a bundle of rough, shaggy, black hair, large, strong features, dark eyes and a broad, crimson, pleasingly asymmetrical mouth. She was, I'm sure, in every sense, conventionally attractive, but what attracted me was her footwear, a pair of spike-heeled, zebra-skin shoes. They were something very special indeed. Her walk was sinuous and not quite steady. That may have been the shoes or she could have been slightly drunk. Drunkenness would explain some of what happened next, but not all of it.

I approached her. She stopped willingly enough and when I asked how many pairs of shoes she had, she said about two hundred and fifty. No doubt my eyes lit up, and I hoped I wasn't drooling. I asked what the shoes were like. She said, and I took it down word for word, 'High heels, peep-toes, ankle straps, a lot of red and black leather, some very soft suede, one or two in silk, some fur mules, some ankle boots, some thigh boots, lots of weird animal skins; you know, your basic set of slut's shoes.'

I felt like all my Christmases had come at once. When I asked if I could photograph her from the ankles down she was delighted. I squatted on the pavement and started shooting the zebra-skin shoes. She moved her feet for me, arching them, turning her ankles this way and that, displaying them for me to admire. She really seemed to be getting into it.

I noticed she had an American accent and I wondered if she was a tourist. People away from home, unsure of the local ground rules, are always more likely to give themselves over to the unexpected. Or perhaps, I thought, Americans are more outgoing, more sexually sophisticated, or maybe they're just more naive. But there was nothing naive about Catherine.

Even though the shoes weren't particularly revealing, I could tell she had really nice feet. They were long and lean and lightly suntanned. All the same, I was unprepared for what I saw when, without my bidding, she kicked off her shoes. Perfection is a difficult concept and it is not a thing you can prove rationally or convince someone else of, nevertheless, as far as I was concerned, the feet that Catherine so casually, so wantonly revealed were absolute perfection. When I saw them bare, their curves and contours, their long elegant toes, their nails lacquered in deep scarlet, when I witnessed the intricate movement of bones and muscles, of veins and skin, I knew they were the feet I had been looking for all my life.

I used up a whole roll of film. They subsequently proved to be excellent photographs. They showed Catherine's beautiful bare feet standing naked on the hot, dusty pavement of South Molton Street, her wonderful zebra-skin shoes lying beside them, expensive, exquisite and so guile-lessly discarded.

She said she had never had a proper foot massage nor a professional pedicure although a couple of her boyfriends had painted her toenails for her. She said she wore high heels for herself and for her men. She said, and I quote again, that they made her feel, 'Potent, dominant and, oh yes, *wet*.'

Then she said as though it had only just occurred to her, 'What are you going to do with those pictures?'

I said they would find a place in my archive.

She laughed. 'So it's not like you're going to take them home and jerk off all over them.'

'Certainly not,' I lied.

We were now at the point in the interview where, in normal circumstances, I would have asked a few offensively intimate questions about her sex life, but I didn't get the chance.

'You're a foot fetishist, right?' she said.

I didn't answer.

'Come on, don't get coy. Feet and shoes turn you on. Yes?'

'All right, yes,' I admitted, and I waited for her to insult me and walk away, but she didn't.

'That's great,' she said. 'I've never met one of those. I mean what do you do? Do you like women to wear shoes while you're fucking them? Do you like to suck their toes? Do you like to be walked on? Come on. Tell me all about it.'

'How long have you got?' I asked.

'All the time in the world.'

So we went to a bar and I told her about it. Not every-thing, that would have taken forever, and, even as it was, it took the rest of the afternoon and some of the evening. But by the end things had changed. By then we had moved on from theory to practice, and again that is not at all what usually happened.

And none of the rest should have happened either. When you approach an unknown woman in the street with the intention of asking her a few mildly obscene questions you might, in your wildest, most optimistic dreams, hope for some kind of sexual liaison; and this we duly, and to my complete astonishment, did have. But you could never, ever hope that such an encounter would present you with the perfect pair of feet. You could not expect to fall in love, and you would certainly never dream of the terrible, violent, appalling consequences that came from that simple, silly, sexually retarded act.

Three

My *Gray's Anatomy* would tell you that the foot is the terminal part of the inferior extremity, what you and I would call the leg. It would say the foot serves as a support structure and also an instrument of locomotion. It would say that the foot is divided into three sections, the tarsus, the metatarsus and the phalanges, that there are seven tarsal bones, five metatarsal bones, fourteen phalangeal bones; a total of twenty-six.

It would say that the foot is intricately and richly supplied with muscles, blood vessels and nerves. Only some of these are responsible for making the foot an object of fascination to a man such as myself.

For instance, on the dorsal surface of the foot you will find the extensor digitorum brevis, a thin broad muscle that subdivides to form four tendons that spread out across the foot. On any foot that I found truly beautiful these tendons would have to be clearly, tautly visible.

Also on that same surface you find the dorsalis pedis artery, a blood vessel which splits and forms branches; namely the tarsea and metatarsea which run parallel across the top of the foot, and the interosseæ and dorsalis hallucis which run along the foot in the direction of the toes. These too stand out in low relief on a beautiful foot.

There are then the cutaneous nerves, the anterior tibial and the saphenous, which criss-cross the foot, again branching and subdividing, interweaving with bone and muscle. These are not obviously visible, yet they are responsible for making the foot so uniquely sensitive.

But an anatomist, for all his knowledge of the structure and internal workings, would not be used to making aesthetic judgements about the foot, whereas I used to spend my whole time doing precisely that.

Let me see if I can describe the perfect pair of women's feet. Certainly they would need to be long and lean. A thick layer of fat around the foot hides its character. They should not be too small and neat in case they look too childlike and innocent, and that is anything but sexy. They should look strong and active. They should have high arches and lean, narrow ankles.

Obviously, these perfect feet will be healthy, free from growths, scars, deformities, without hard or discoloured or flaky skin. However, I am not averse to a foot having a lived-in look. A lifetime of wearing high heels and exotic shoes will inevitably leave a few traces, and these are not to be despised.

The flesh may be stark white or beautifully tanned, but as I say, in either case, the bones, tendons and veins must be visible through the skin, rippling and articulating as the foot moves. Occasionally one sees a foot that looks as taut and veined as an engorged penis. Or is it the other way round? That is the kind of foot I lust over. That is the kind of foot Catherine had.

The toes need to be long, straight and slender. They should never be plump or bulbous. Twisted or overlapping toes are hideous, and, despite the examples we see in Renaissance and Greek sculpture, I like the first toe to be shorter than the big toe.

The nails are all-important. The perfectly shaped foot can

be ruined by bad nails, and the prime factor here is shape. They must not be spatulate. They should be the shape of tiny television screens rather than of sea shells. They should be large in relation to the size of the toe, centrally and symmetrically placed. They should be without ridges and free from cuticle debris. They should be kept long rather than cut short and of course they should be painted. The range of acceptable colours runs a comparatively narrow spectrum, from dark pink to deep maroon, and my personal preference is for something approaching Porsche red. White, silver, metallic and pearl finishes are totally dreadful. I always think that black polish should deliver a certain frisson, yet I find it never quite does. Greens and purples seem merely odd and unnatural, and, if it seems strange to talk about nature in this cosmetic context, I think that what we're actually dealing with here is nature red in claw if not in tooth.

Foot jewellery has always struck me as a gilding of the lily. Likewise painting the feet with henna seems an unnecessary, and not especially sexual, complication. I can see that a small tattoo on the foot could have a certain erotic charge, but I have always felt that the perfect foot would not be tattooed, and Catherine's feet certainly were not.

I realize, of course, that laying down laws for female beauty is an absurd and dangerous occupation. And if I sound dogmatic and impossibly demanding, all I can say is sorry but that's how it is with fetishes. Of course, feet that do not conform to my ideal have every right to exist, have every right to be admired. Indeed I myself have admired and been intimate with feet that were a long way from perfect. Nevertheless, a man knows what he wants. And in one sense I am being descriptive rather than prescriptive, for, as I describe my idea of the perfect foot, I find that I am very precisely describing Catherine's.

But the perfect foot is not bare. It is shod. The shoe delivers a vital aesthetic transformation. It customizes a part of the body. Whereas the perfect foot allows only one possibility, there are an infinite number of shoes that may be admired and enjoyed. And finding the right shoe is the comparatively easy part. Shoes can be bought, they can be specially made, whereas the perfect foot is a natural phenomenon like the Grand Canyon or the Victoria Falls.

Of course the shoes need to be high heeled, the higher the better within reason. I don't personally feel any need to psychoanalyse the high heel but undoubtedly it makes women stand and walk differently. It raises their buttocks and it makes them wiggle. It makes them look dominant but at the same time it makes them quite vulnerable. It is hard for them to run away. Hence the term 'fuck-me shoes', or FMs as I prefer to call them; i.e., the woman is saying if you can catch me you can fuck me, and of course, any damn fool can catch a woman in a pair of shoes with six-inch heels.

This does not sound politically correct, I know; indeed it sounds downright misogynistic, but, hey, I didn't invent the term or the concept. As a matter of fact, the first time I ever saw the phrase 'fuck-me shoes' in print was in Shelley Winters' autobiography, *Shelley, Sometimes Known as Shirley*.

She tells how, in her early career, she and Marilyn Monroe used to steal shoes from the studio to go dancing in. They were high-heeled sandals with a kind of lattice work at the toe and an ankle strap tied in a bow, and she refers to them as fuck-me shoes. She says, 'They really were the sexiest shoes I've ever seen.'

Like Shelley, I'm a great fan of the ankle strap, and even more so of the double ankle strap. I'm absolutely sure this must have something to do with bondage and restraint, and it is echoed in thongs, and even in certain kinds of laces. All these are very welcome.

Fabrics may vary, but only within certain limits. I tend to like my women's shoes to be made of something that was once alive; leather or suede, snake or alligator-skin, tiger, antelope or, as in Catherine's case, zebra. But I am not too dogmatic about this. I also enjoy velvet, silk and satin. Synthetic fabrics are not a source of pleasure for me. Perspex, plastic, Bakelite are not on my erotic map, and neither are raffia, wood or rubber.

Colour is again important. My taste is towards strong colours, reds and blacks above all, but purples and blues are fine too. Earth tones, beiges, yellows and greys are really not on at all, and white shoes are, of course, simply absurd.

I am something of a classicist in my choice of shoes. I like them to be bold and uncluttered. I go for the grand sweep rather than the telling detail. I like them to be hard-edged, smooth, streamlined. I really don't have much time for fussiness, for buckles and bows, buttons, beadwork, rhinestones, sequins, artificial flowers. On the other hand, I am very prepared to be entertained by a mule, a slingback, a strappy sandal, a fur slipper. Much as I like the straight stiletto, I am still an admirer of the comma heel and the *talon choc*.

There is, however, a whole category of shoe that is simply unerotic. Included here are the clog, the trainer, the flip-flop, the Dr Scholl exercise sandal. We need not concern ourselves with these except to note that my dislike of them indicates the extent to which my fetishism is concerned with aesthetics, not with function or proximity. It's not the *idea* of the foot or shoe that's important to me, it's the reality, the sight, the touch, the form.

I have nothing against boots, whether they run to the ankle, to the calf, the knee or the thigh, and I'm well aware that a whole category of fetishist worships them. But they fail to work for me simply because they enclose and therefore hide the foot. They conceal the object of desire. This might be a good thing if one's sexual partner had ugly feet, I suppose, but how could you live with such a partner? How could you have sex with her?

What a good shoe crucially does, must do, is *reveal* the foot, enhance and display it, offer a frame and a setting for it. And this is precisely the nature of my erotic obsession. I crave the intersection of art and nature, of the human body and the created object, the foot and the shoe, flesh and leather.

I am not one of those unhealthy fetishists who will curl up at night masturbating into a black silk slingback. I need a female presence to give life to the shoe. And I need a shoe to embellish and fully eroticize the foot.

I must admit that in all these calculations I find myself envisaging a white foot in a dark shoe, and I hope this doesn't sound racist, or more precisely, I suppose, 'skinist'. Frankly, I don't see why it should. I'm talking about preference here, not prejudice. But a black-skinned foot in a dark shoe lacks contrast and tension, and the same applies to a black foot with dark-painted nails. You might then think that a dark foot in a white shoe or with white-painted nails would be erotic, but for me those things don't hit the pleasure centres at all.

There is one area where dark skin is infinitely more dramatic than white and that is in the matter of sperm. White strands and globs of semen standing out against a background of a taut black instep is an immensely powerful and moving image, however it seems somehow peripheral to the true stuff of foot and shoe fetishism. It may involve a foot, but it is somehow not *about* that foot.

Rather, for me, the entire nexus of foot and shoe sexuality is emblemized by the peep-toe. Ah, the peep-toe, that most perverse and erotic element of all. The foot is partly concealed by the body of the shoe, but here at its very apex we have a small, circular, inviting orifice. The bare flesh of the big toe is indecently revealed, ready to be touched or kissed, pushing out through this hole, penis-like, no doubt, mimicking penetration, the toenail varnished a glossy, vibrant, cherry red. The erotic charge of the peep-toe is more potent, exciting and dangerous than anything I know. Catherine wore a lot of peep-toed shoes.

Four

The above was part, but only a small part, of what I told Catherine that evening in the bar on the day we met. She was genuinely fascinated. She found it strange, and perhaps slightly shocking, but she certainly wasn't repelled. As she said, she had never encountered a real foot and shoe fetishist before, and she found me interesting, a curiosity, a case study. She was attracted by the fact that I was different, and perhaps she was attracted by other things too. I am a reasonably good-looking man. I have a certain charm and openness. She was interested to meet a fetishist but I don't think she would have gone drinking with me had I been physically repellent, if I had been older or uglier or if I had more closely resembled the popular image of a sexual pervert. The fact that I do not resemble this image is not the least of my advantages. She was also an American, and, strange as it seems to me, some Americans still have a taste for things British. She said she was 'attached to the university', whatever that meant, and perhaps I was an area of research for her.

At some point in our long session in the bar it became inevitable that we would go home together, the only doubt being whose home. For my part I wanted very much to go to hers. There was the promise of two hundred and fifty pairs of fuck-me shoes, and for her there was the security of being on her own territory. She needed a little persuading, but in the end she shrugged and agreed.

We arrived by taxi, thickly drunk by now. Her flat was rented and looked curiously unlived-in, very unhomely. She said she hadn't been there long, wasn't sure if she was staying. As an American in London it fitted. I supposed she was just passing through. That should have made me suspicious. We soon found our way into her bedroom. My imagination had been working too hard, accelerating away. I had pictured all two hundred and fifty pairs of shoes artfully displayed on shelves, shown to their best advantage, spotlit like exotic birds. She saw me looking around, saw my confusion and disappointment.

'I lied,' she said quietly.

My disappointment increased, no doubt tinged with drunken frustration and anger. It had never occurred to me that she was a liar, much less a tease.

'I was drunk,' she continued. 'I just thought of a number and tripled it.'

I made a move towards the door, towards leaving.

'Hey, I'm sorry,' she said. 'It was just a joke. I don't have two hundred and fifty pairs. But I do have one or two good pairs of shoes if you want to see them. If you want me to dress up in them.'

She could see that I didn't believe her. She had committed an act of betrayal. I felt used and deceived, and I wasn't going to make myself vulnerable again so quickly.

In a corner of the room there was a large oak wardrobe that had a deep drawer along the full width of its base. She pulled it open, trying to be conciliatory, trying to please. Inside there were some shoe boxes, though scarcely more than half a dozen. I knew that quality and quantity were not the same thing, nevertheless I wasn't expecting much, but she opened the boxes one by one, and in the end I was partly consoled. She did own some very elegant and pleasing pairs of shoes; a pair of Manolo Blahnik evening mules in red satin, a pair of Maud Frizon high heels in black suede with open backs, a pair of towering black patent stilettos from Frederick's of Hollywood, a pair of trashy Terry de Havilland platforms in what looked like gold snake-skin, some very curious Kurt Geiger open sandals with a tripod heel, three slender metal supports converging in an inverted cone like a piece of miniature scaffolding. The feeling of being let down had hardly passed, but these shoes weren't at all bad. I was quietly impressed and I was prepared to be forgiving. At least now we could have sex.

The question of what foot and shoe fetishists do in bed isn't a particularly complex one. Nor is it difficult to answer. They do everything that everybody else does, but they do one or two other things as well. They (we) use all the techniques and actions and positions that everyone else does, but usually the woman is wearing high heels.

The fetishist will fondle his partner's feet, of course. He will kiss them, perhaps lick and suck the toes. The woman will run her feet, whether shod or bare, over her partner's body. Of course she will concentrate on his erogenous zones, of course she will use her feet to massage his genitals, she may well press her feet into his face.

The practice of taking your partner's toes in your mouth is known to some people as 'shrimping', and in one sense this seems like rather a good term. The toes do resemble shrimps by virtue of being pink, curled and soft, and of about the right size. But the word shrimping sounds like a frivolous and silly activity, and when I have a woman's toes in my mouth, the feeling is anything but frivolous. For me it is a moment of breathtaking, stomach-churning intensity.

In answer to a question Catherine asked right at the

beginning, I was able to assure her that I had no desire to be walked on, trodden on, or kicked. There's a certain undeniable element of self-abasement involved in scrabbling around at a woman's feet, but humiliation and subjugation are no part of my own sexual profile, although I'm sure there are other foot and shoe fetishists for whom they're essential.

So that is what Catherine and I did together – all the usual things. We were drunk and we were unfamiliar with each other's tastes and preferences, the very conditions that make a first time so exciting yet so unsatisfactory.

Despite having a few, though extremely limited number of, pairs of shoes to choose from, and despite her willingness to explore this new sexual area, when it came right down to it I asked her to keep on the zebra-skin numbers she'd been wearing in the street. After all, they were the ones that had brought us together. In fact they weren't a famous make. There was no signature or manufacturer's name inside, just a small trade mark, the outline of a bare footprint with a tiny lightning flash across it. It wasn't a mark I recognized, so I made a note to look it up when I got back to my archive. I asked her where she'd bought them and she said in a second-hand clothes shop in Islington, but they had been unworn.

I stayed the night, and the next morning, early, a little hungover, a little shamefaced, having received no offer of breakfast, I said goodbye. We exchanged telephone numbers, but I couldn't tell if Catherine was being anything other than polite.

At some point in the night I had asked her whether this was the sort of thing she did very often, allowing herself to be picked up in the street by strange men. It was a crass question, I know.

'What do you want me to say?' she demanded. 'That I've never done anything remotely like this before, not once, not ever. That you're so special, so attractive, so charismatic, that I was driven to do something dangerous and out of character that I'd never normally do.'

Now, I am sufficiently versed in the arts and science of courtship to realize that it's no good simply telling a woman that she has perfect feet, the feet you've been looking for all your life, feet that you could happily spend the rest of your life contemplating, adoring, worshipping. You just can't do that, certainly not on a first date. It just scares them away, and I was determined that Catherine should not be scared.

Given the strange, unlikely way we had got together, neither of us had any right to expect anything from the other. The situation, the transaction, had all the features of a brief and singular encounter, a one-night stand, but I knew from the very beginning that I wanted it to be much more than that. It is not every day you encounter the perfect feet of your dreams, and when you do, you aren't inclined to let them skip away so easily.

I stood on the threshold of her flat, about to let myself out. She stood at the other end of the hall, across an expanse of marble tiles, and it was quite clear that she was not about to kiss me goodbye. She had a chaste blue robe wrapped around her, but she was barefoot. I saw nothing chaste in that. I half-slid, half-pounced the length of the hall, and threw myself at her feet. I gave them a final ravish before I left. Above me I heard her give a small, dry laugh, and at the time I chose to believe her laughter was not unkind.

Five

I think it's important to say right away that I perceive myself as a serious person. I read newspapers. I follow politics. I try to keep up with the new books and films, plays and exhibitions. In my interactions with the world, in my job (which is dull but responsible), in my tastes and opinions and beliefs, I would say that I'm a substantial and complete and serious person. Yet I can see that there is something profoundly unserious about being a foot and shoe fetishist.

Certain sexual obsessions, let us say an addiction to pain, either given or received, a taste for violation of the self or others, a compulsive attraction towards children or animals or faeces, these things carry with them a sense of scale, of drama, of awful consequence, that a love of feet and shoes simply does not.

This is a paradox and occasionally a problem. Here I am, this serious person, seriously obsessed with something that most people are unable to take seriously. Tell people you are obsessed with bondage, with cottaging, with prostitutes and see them react. They may express surprise or shock or disapproval, and this expression may be real or feigned, it may be only an attempt to hide their true feelings, it may be a conditioned response, but either way there *is* a definite response. They look at you as though you're talking about something risky and edgy and, yes, serious. But tell them you're a foot fetishist and they giggle. For them it's a joke, it's funny, it's not serious sex. Yet for me it is. For me it is the only kind of serious sex.

For a long time I wasn't sure whether I was a fetishist or a partialist. This is an important distinction. A partialist is someone who likes, who is attracted to a nice pair of feet or shoes; he enjoys them and they add to his sexual pleasure, but they are not *necessary* for that pleasure, whereas a true fetishist needs the shoes or feet in order to derive any sexual pleasure at all. The presence of the fetish object is a necessary precondition before sexual activity can even take place.

Personally I'm quite sure that I *could* make love to a woman who had ordinary or even unattractive feet, or to a woman who was wearing dreary or ugly shoes (so in that sense it might be argued that I'm not a true fetishist at all); but why should I? The bottom line is I really don't think I could be *bothered* to make love to a woman whose feet I didn't find attractive. There are enough pairs of attractive feet and shoes in the world that you simply don't need to force yourself to make love to someone who doesn't possess them.

I didn't always feel this way. I wasn't always like this. It has all been slide and slippage, a slow ascent or descent, I'm not sure which, on some sexual escalator, or a rudderless drift downstream over treacherous waters, a path of least resistance, not that I would ever have wanted to resist.

I was once more or less orthodox in my relations with women. I went out on dates. I went to parties. I met women in the course of my work and my social life. I talked to them, went out with them, enjoyed their company, went to bed with them, had fun sometimes, was serious about them sometimes. It was OK, but it was rarely *more* than

OK. It was usually not quite right. I never found exactly what I was looking for, because for a long time I didn't know what I was looking for, and even when I did know there was a time when I wasn't prepared to admit it.

I had always known that I was attracted to women who had good feet. I knew I liked women who wore good shoes. I knew I liked them a lot, a lot more than I liked women who didn't have good feet, who didn't wear good shoes. But I tried to pretend that feet and shoes weren't my only interests. And to some extent that wasn't entirely a pretence. I liked women with good breasts and good legs and good minds too. These things were attractive and appealing. I could even see that they were desirable, but they were never necessary. And if anyone had asked me how I felt about feet and shoes I would have said I felt fine about them. I would have been prepared to admit to being a partialist, even though a part of me always wanted to admit to something more.

There was no road to Damascus experience about it, no crucial moment, no trauma. I simply decided to concentrate and focus. I gradually realized I'd had enough of all that relationship nonsense. I knew I couldn't go on the way I had been, seeing women who didn't quite hit the spot, so I decided to take the plunge. I decided to go to hell in a shoe box. I would stop pretending. I would stop being a partialist. I'd go the whole hog and throw myself into proper foot and shoe fetishism. I would stop looking for a woman with a good personality or a good complexion. I would not be averse to these things, but they would be only peripheral pleasures. Feet were what really mattered.

You might think that in doing this I had abandoned a part of my humanity, that being a fetishist involved some kind of demeaning bondage. Wrong. What I felt I had abandoned was all the dead wood, the window dressing. I was getting down to essentials, and for me it was a supreme liberation. When I met a woman, a prospective sexual partner, there would be no more conversations about what films we'd seen, what music we liked, what hopes and plans we had for the future, where we liked to spend our holidays. There would be no more worries about where the relationship was 'going'. All I needed was a woman with a great pair of feet. She didn't even need to have great shoes. I'd be only too happy to provide those for her. It seemed to me that my decision, my admission, would make life much easier for all concerned.

I continued to lead what I considered to be a normal life, the only difference being that I now knew what I wanted. I looked unashamedly at women and their feet. I started to amass material for my archive. And every so often I'd do something a little bit eccentric. I'd hang around outside women's shoe shops, looking at the shoes in the window and looking through into the store at the women putting shoes on and taking them off. And once in a while I'd spot a great-looking pair of feet walking along the street and I'd follow them for a couple of miles. And just once in a while I'd go out on the streets with a clipboard and ask women questions about their feet and shoes.

The problem remained, however, that, even given my concentration on finding the one thing I needed, tracking down a woman who possessed a pair of feet that measured up to the erotic model in my head was always going to be extremely difficult. There were a number of near misses, a number of occasions when I made do with feet that were less than my ideal, that were good but not great. But I never got depressed, and I never doubted that sooner or later I would find what I was looking for. It had been a long hard search that had brought me to Catherine, but that only added to my satisfaction, to my determination not to lose her.

I let two whole days pass before I telephoned her, a feat that required considerable restraint, self-discipline and self-denial, not resources that I normally have in any abundance. Even when I decided it was time to phone I had no confidence that it would be easy to make contact with her again. She did not look like the sort of woman who sat by her phone waiting for it to ring. But I called and she was there and she answered.

'I wondered if and when you'd call,' she said.

'Did you want me to?'

'I don't know.'

That was not the answer I was looking for. I wanted her to know. I wanted her to say that she'd been waiting impatiently, counting the hours, willing me to call. I knew that was too much to expect, but even so I had hoped for more warmth in her voice, more of an indication that she was glad to hear from me.

'So, how are you?' I asked.

'I'm fine, I guess.'

'And how are those feet of yours?'

A pause before she said, 'I guess they're fine too.'

There was a hint of amusement in her voice. I hoped that was a good sign. I hoped it didn't mean that she found my enquiry absurd.

'Don't they need stroking?' I asked. 'Or massaging or kissing or fondling?'

'I don't know,' she said.

'Don't you?'

'No. I really don't.'

'I could come over and do all that for you now,' I said,

35

trying to make it sound like a generous and harmless offer, trying not to sound too adolescently eager.

'I know you could,' she replied.

'I want to.'

'I expect you do. But I'm not sure.'

There was no point in pressing too hard, in scaring her off. I waited and said nothing, hoping that would force her to speak. The silence that followed was confusing and uncommitted. I knew she didn't want to give me a straight answer, that she didn't simply want to say yes, but I was encouraged by the fact that she said nothing at all, since that meant at least she wasn't saying no.

'I just don't know,' was what she finally said.

'OK then, just meet me for a drink.'

I thought a drink sounded uncomplicated enough, but she still wouldn't say yes. Another oblique silence ensued and I was determined not to break it.

At last she was forced to say something. She said, 'Look, I try to live in the real world. It's not always easy but I'm not dumb. I'm not looking for true love. I know what it's like out there. I know some relationships are about sex and nothing else. That's OK. I've had relationships like that, they're fine, they make sense to me. I like the excitement. I like men who are different, unusual. I just wonder if maybe you're a little too unusual for me.'

This was difficult to deal with. If I said I wasn't unusual at all, which was how I felt about myself, then that was apparently no recommendation. However, if I insisted that I really was wildly unusual, then I was in danger of confirming her fears.

Lamely I said, 'The more you get to know me, the less unusual I'll seem.'

'I don't know that I want to get to know you.'

'Why not?'

'It's too complicated.'

'If getting to know me is too complicated then don't get to know me. Just meet me. Just have a drink. Just have sex.'

She laughed. 'I'm not trying to be difficult,' she said, and I could almost believe her. 'But I think I have a problem. When you were here the other morning, in the hall just before you left, when you knelt at my feet and kissed them, when I felt your tongue on my skin, your saliva on my toes, it felt very strange indeed. It felt crazy and stupid and absurd. And it also felt horny as hell.'

I kept silent but I knew that something had changed, that she had said something important, something she had perhaps not wanted to say. She had made a confession.

'I've been thinking about it ever since,' she added. 'I've been masturbating about it ever since.'

'So what are you telling me?'

'I don't know. I guess I'm telling you, OK, I'll meet you for a drink.'

We met in a dark, subterranean wine bar. There were gnarled candles in bottles, sawdust on the floor, pieces of archaic wine-making equipment mounted on the hessian walls. It was hot, dark and crowded, and the noise of other people's conversation was intrusive. We sat in a brick arch, at a small, unstable circular table, and got quietly drunk, and we talked in a way that didn't threaten us with the dangers of getting to know each other too well. We found each other easy enough to talk to, but the conversation was all subtext, the real exchange of language was going on below the level of the table.

Catherine was wearing the Maud Frizon, open-backed, suede court shoes. The heels were slender and tapered and there was one black strip of suede that ran across the top of the foot. From time to time I reached down and held her feet, ran my finger slowly along the lines where flesh and suede met. In return she occasionally ran her foot up the inside of my thigh to my genitals where she applied a firm but teasing pressure with the sole of her shoe. The pleasure was honeyed and restricted and tense, and I was gradually losing control. The next time her right foot came within reach I closed my hand round the black suede shoe and pulled it off. I stroked the ball of Catherine's foot and she smiled in feline pleasure, but after a moment or two I stopped, and she was surprised to see me slip the shoe into my pocket and get up from the table. I crossed the wine bar purposefully, performing body swerves around the backs of chairs and gaggles of drinkers, and when I was clear I entered the toilets, but I was not gone long. When I returned, I handed the shoe back to Catherine. I did it quite openly across the table and there was a possibility that the people around us might have seen me do it.

Perplexed, she took the shoe from me and looked inside. She could see that it was wet. A long, thick, lacy trail of semen ran down the slope of the leather inner sole. In a cubicle in the toilet I had masturbated into her shoe. She stared at the strange, indecent juxtaposition of suede, leather lining and bodily fluid. She looked at me, and it was a look I could not wholly interpret. It would have been easy to read anger and distaste into her gaze, but there was also excitement and pleasure. She shook her head, showed disbelief, at me, and the situation and at herself. She pulled a sharp snort of breath in through her nostrils, and then she reached down and slid her foot into the shoe again.

I watched her face, imagining the sensations she must be experiencing; the warm, dense semen pressed beneath her heel, on her sole, spreading, seeping into the crevices between her toes, creating a thin adhesion. And then I saw her slide a hand under her dress and I watched as she touched herself for the briefest moment before her features tightened and her eyes looked away to signal a brief, fierce orgasm.

Almost immediately she regained her composure, straightened herself and said, 'I'm not sure that I know what the fuck I'm doing here.'

I said, 'It looked like you were having a very good time.'

That made no impression. Ignoring me, she continued, 'I don't know what the fuck I'm doing letting you masturbate into my shoe, playing with myself in public. I don't know what this is all about.'

'I could try to explain,' I said.

'Could you? I'm not sure that you could.'

'I could try.'

So we ordered another drink and I tried.

Six

I have never been much of a student, certainly never much of a scholar. The world of learning, of libraries and texts, of specialized knowledge, of references and cross-references, of bibliographies and databases, has in general meant very little to me. The world of Theory means even less. Yet, partly through force of circumstances, partly through choice, I have become a scholar of my own condition. I have read the required texts. I have tried to cover the material. I have annotated. I have set up my archive. (Of which, more later.) I have tried to keep up to date. I have become an authority, if not a wholly reliable one. Above all, I have tried to understand myself.

I believe it was Krafft-Ebing who first used the term fetishism in the sense that we understand it today. His *Psychopathia Sexualis* is full of stories about foot and shoe fetishism and I have read them with some pleasure; stories of men forced to keep pairs of boots hidden in bed so they can fondle them and become aroused enough to get an erection with their wives, stories of men who take chickens along to their favourite prostitutes and get them to trample the birds to death in their high-heeled boots.

Krafft-Ebing is always a good read, but unfortunately he was a forensic psychologist, so he only ever became involved when a crime was committed. He may well have come across healthy, well-adjusted fetishists who led sane, normal lives, but they weren't part of his work and they didn't really interest him. What, I wonder, would he have made of me? Of course, I like to think he would have made nothing at all. He would have looked at me, looked at my behaviour and seen no problem. Freud, however, might have seen it very differently.

Freud, of course, has a theory about fetishism and it's a cracker. He says that the young male child believes that everyone, male and female, has a penis, just like him. That sounds fair enough. How would he know any different? But, says Freud, a moment comes when he finally sees a naked woman, and straight away he spots that she doesn't have a penis after all. The little boy is shocked and appalled. Someone seems to have lopped off the woman's penis. And he realizes the same thing could happen to him. So, symbolically, he needs to provide her with a phallus, or at least a phallic substitute, a fetish object. In this traumatic moment he looks frantically around him, sees a pair of shoes lying on the floor or sees the woman's naked feet, and thinks that'll do nicely. A fetishist is born.

Can Freud really mean it? Can he really believe this explains anything? I mean, I fear castration as much as the next man but I don't see how that results in a desire to attach penises to people who never had them in the first place. And I'm especially worried about the part that says the fetish object is something the patient saw at the same moment that he saw his first female genitals.

My guess is that a fair percentage of males must get their first glimpse of the female genitals either in a bedroom or a bathroom. I will admit that shoes may well be present in these places, and they're conveniently situated, they are (arguably) more or less phallic shaped. But it's easy to think of plenty of other things that would be present too; loofahs, bath taps, shower heads, bars of soap, all of which seem every bit as phallic as shoes, all of which would be equally good (or bad) phallic substitutes, and yet one doesn't hear of too many soap or loofah fetishists.

Now, not even Freud's worst enemies would say that he really thought this whole business through. But I think the clear implication of his ideas is that when I'm lusting after a woman's foot, I'm actually lusting after a penis. As I have said before, I do like feet that are large, veiny and rippled, that have an appearance that might, I suppose, be regarded as quasi-phallic. And it's true that I sometimes suck a woman's big toe in much the same way that some people suck a penis. But both these are imperfect analogies. The foot is only *somewhat* like a penis. Neither foot nor big toe is erectile, neither is a similar size or shape to an actual penis, neither is capable of ejaculation.

More to the point, what tells me that Freud didn't get it quite right is the fact that when I'm fondling or kissing a foot, I have no desire to be fondling a penis. And if, by some chance, I was presented with a penis, and if I sucked it, this would not be at all the same thing as sucking a woman's foot. It would not be nearly so pleasurable. It would not satisfy any of my sexual desires. Freud thinks the foot may be a substitute for the penis, but I am here to tell him that the penis is no substitute for the foot.

Another, equally unconvincing theory is that fetishism is all about weaning. The baby is torn unwillingly from the breast. Denied what he wants, the baby is set down on the floor, down where the shoes and feet are. He looks about him for a substitute, and lo and behold he discovers feet. I find this an ingenious theory but I'm even less inclined to believe it than I am Freud. The foot and shoe seem even less convincing as a surrogate breast than they do as a surrogate penis.

The main problem I have in considering these explanations is that, inevitably, I just don't have any memories of these formative experiences. I certainly don't remember the beginning or end of my weaning. No doubt I was dismayed to be taken away from the nipple, no doubt I wanted more, but did I really lie there on the Axminster and cast about for a substitute breast? Is that why I'm the way I am? I just don't know, but it seems unlikely.

I'm no clearer on when I saw my first naked woman. I don't remember even seeing my mother naked. There were no sisters in the house, no precocious cousins or neighbourhood girls who ever played doctors and nurses with me. There were no visits to nudist beaches. I may have seen a few nude statues when I was a child, and later I certainly saw girly magazines. They were strange and confusing documents at the best of times, but I don't think I tried, either psychically or otherwise, to provide these shockingly exposed women with a penis. It does occur to me that some of the women in the girly magazines were likely to have been wearing fancy high heels, but I can't make anything out of that.

When I talk of Krafft-Ebing or Freud I am probably showing the limitations of my knowledge. There is a lot of new discussion about sexuality, and though I try my best to keep up with it, I don't find it easy. Feminists for example are very het up about fetishism for all kinds of reasons. To start with, they're not happy with the old definitions. If you take Freud's line that the fetish object is a penis substitute it means that women can't be fetishists. They don't need to psychically provide men with phalluses because men already physically have them. And this makes feminists

43

unhappy. They don't like the idea that they can't be fetishists. They don't want to be denied an option that's available
to men. But they're also unhappy with the whole idea that
sex is solely about penises, and I tend to share their feelings.

One strain of feminism tends to believe that the accepted
norms of heterosexuality and heterosexual society operate
to repress women. Therefore, they reason, anything that
disturbs those norms and that society must be a good thing.
I'm not at all sure how I feel about this. I can see that the
wilder shores of sexuality do seem to threaten many of the
norms that our society holds dear, but I'm not sure if fetishism fits into that category. I think foot and shoe fetishism
is an essentially conservative form.

For one thing it seems to be as old as civilization. But far
more to the point, as far as I can see, it threatens nobody
and nothing. It can coexist with marriage, with family life,
with religion (whether organized or unorganized), with
capitalism or socialism, or any other damn political system.

I don't think of myself as inherently conservative, but I
suppose I am to the extent that I quite like the world I live
in. It presents enough opportunities for me to enjoy my
obsession. There might be other worlds in which those
opportunities would be more numerous and my enjoyment
greater and, yes, I find that an attractive idea, but I'm not
basically dissatisfied with the current state of play.

Or put it another way; perhaps there is a Utopian society
to be found somewhere, a supposedly happier and healthier
place, a place in which all sexual neurosis has been allevi-
ated, where fetishism and deviation and perversion are
wholly absent. But if so, well, thanks very much but I
wouldn't want to live there. I'm happy in the here and
now, with my fetishism.

It seems to me that almost all male sexuality is fetishized

to a greater or lesser extent. However catholic we may be in our sexual tastes we still have preferences. Even those men who claim to 'love all women' must still love some women more than others, which is to say they prefer women who possess certain qualities to the exclusion of certain other qualities. Is a man who demands a high IQ in a woman any different from a man who demands a good pair of feet? I don't think so.

I have a feeling this may be what all sex and even all love is about. When we say, 'I love her because she is kind,' we are separating her kindness from all her other attributes. However much we love the whole person it's not possible to love all a person's attributes equally. However much we love someone there are always things about them that we like more than others. 'I love her strength but not her short temper, her good humour but not her docility.' We are all fetishists in these matters.

Why should that surprise us? We live in a fetishized society. We are accustomed to take the part for the whole. We are beset with graven images. We see a man driving a Rolls-Royce. We see a woman in a Chanel suit. We see someone consulting their Rolex. Is this really any different from seeing a woman in a pair of fuck-me shoes? It is not only in the sexual arena that objects speak more concisely and eloquently about people than they could ever speak for themselves.

I tried to talk about this with Catherine, and at least in the beginning she appeared to be interested, but I could feel myself sinking. The moment I said anything, the moment I asserted anything as true, it felt like a silly generalization and its opposite could be equally true.

In a last, slightly desperate, bid to make her understand I said how much simpler fetishism could make life. I said it had not been easy to find a woman with a perfect pair of feet but it had at least been possible. I had at last succeeded. If I had been looking for the perfect soulmate, someone who conformed to the idealized specifications of romantic love or spiritual need, I might have been looking for the rest of my life. Finding a woman who was perfect in one way was hard enough. How could one expect to find someone who was perfect in every way. What's more, I insisted, having someone like me could make life much easier for the woman too. 'Just keep your feet in good shape and wear the right shoes,' I said, 'and I'll love you forever.'

That was the first time she looked really unhappy. That use of the word love really scared her.

'You know,' she said, 'I think you may be a very crazy person.'

Seven

But she was wrong. In those days, as I have said, I was not a crazy person at all. And if more proof were needed of my sanity, of my essential social adequacy, I would have presented my friends. I had plenty of them; friends from work, friends from university, even the odd remaining friend from school. I had male friends and female friends, friends in couples, single friends, married friends, friends in ménages, the occasional gay friend. And especially I had Mike and Natasha. Mike and Natasha were nice people and they liked me. If I had been a true degenerate they couldn't possibly have wanted me as their friend.

I had been at university with both of them. They met in their first year and had been together ever since. They were my best friends, both of them equally. I was fond of them and they were fond of me. They led a secure, comfortable, affluent, couply sort of life, and that was just fine by me. There was nothing there for me to disapprove of. In fact, most of the time I was extremely envious. I had no problem with the way they lived their lives, but I sensed they had a problem with the way I lived mine.

To their credit, I'm sure this came out of compassion and concern. They seemed to think I must be unhappy, or perhaps that I *ought* to be unhappy, since I wasn't leading a secure, comfortable, couply sort of life like them. They thought I had a little problem that needed solving. They weren't unsympathetic, they just wished it would go away. I know they must have speculated from time to time about why I was still single, why I'd never even lived with anyone, why I'd never made it to the sort of life they'd got. Essentially, I think they just wished I was more 'settled'.

In the beginning I used to introduce my girlfriends to Mike and Natasha, and they tried very hard to like them, even the ones I didn't particularly like myself. They were always warm and welcoming, they were like that. We went out together in foursomes, did things, had meals together. But I think Mike and Natasha eventually found the emotional investment too much. They'd pin all their hopes on some new woman who'd entered my life, then a month later they'd have to start all over again. Using methods of greater or lesser subtlety, they sometimes tried to find out what was going wrong.

'Are you not seeing Angela any more?' Mike would ask.

'That's right.'

Mike would be prepared to leave it at that but Natasha would ask, 'Why not?'

I'd shrug and say, 'You know how it is.'

'No,' said Natasha. 'Tell me.'

Trying to make a joke of it I'd reply, 'She wasn't Miss Right.'

Taking me more seriously than I wanted to take myself, Natasha would ask, 'What does Miss Right look like?'

'I don't know. I haven't met her yet.'

'Will you know her when you do?'

'Sure.'

'So what are the qualities she'll have?'

Even then I could have talked about admiring a person's qualities as being a form of fetishization, but mercifully I didn't. At this point, sensing my discomfort, Mike would step in and say, 'Hey, give the man a break.'

'He doesn't mind,' Natasha would say. 'You don't mind, do you?'

'No,' I'd say, though I suppose I did mind.

'See, he doesn't mind.'

'I think it'll be an instinctive kind of thing,' I'd say.

'Instinctive?'

'Yes, like goalkeeping.'

'Goalkeeping. Right. Well, thanks for clearing that one up for us.'

They liked to think I was incorrigible. They even had a spell of trying to introduce me to suitable women. I didn't mind that particularly. My life was never so full of women that I wasn't glad to meet one or two more, especially since these women had been screened by Mike and Natasha and deemed suitable. There was always the possibility that one of them would have great feet. But they never did.

I'd meet them, talk to them, be friendly, and the evening would go well enough, but since I was being encouraged to think of these women as potential partners and mates, I had to check their feet. And their feet were never the feet of my dreams. I can't remember the exact chapter and verse, their foot and shoe failings were not so hideous as to be permanently imprinted in my memory, but I know they were never any good.

'Would you like Sarah's phone number?' Natasha asked.

'No thanks.'

'Why not?'

'Because I don't want to phone her.'

'Why not?'

'Because I don't want to talk to her.'

49

'What's wrong with her? What's wrong with all my friends?'

'Nothing,' I said. 'It's probably something wrong with me.'

Mike put on his German psychiatrist accent. 'Now ziss is very interesting.'

But while I didn't want to satisfy their curiosity, I don't deny that I was flattered by their interest in me. I liked being a source of fascination and speculation and concern. Mike always pretended to disapprove of Natasha's prying but I knew he was as nosy as she was.

It wouldn't have been impossible to tell them that I was a foot and shoe fetishist. I felt sure they wouldn't have been horrified, and I wouldn't have been particularly embarrassed, but I never wanted to. It was simply more enjoyable if it was a part of my life that I kept to myself.

So they stopped trying to find suitable girls for me, and I stopped introducing my succession of transitory girlfriends. It suited us all fine. Mike and Natasha knew plenty of other couples but I never felt very at home with them, so when we met up it tended to be just the three of us. We were capable of doing quite blokish things together, like going to the pub to play pool or going to watch Sunday League cricket. Other times we'd be cultured and go to see new films or plays or concerts. I always felt very at ease in their company and I'd never, never felt like a gooseberry.

Occasionally Mike would turn to me and say something like, 'How about we ditch the wife, score some cocaine, pick up a couple of harlots and shag our brains out in a sordid hovel in King's Cross?'

But, hey, I knew he didn't mean it. Given that Mike and Natasha had been together for about ten years, and given that they were perfectly normal people, and despite the fact that they obviously adored each other, I did wonder if they had stayed wholly faithful to each other all that time. It was only human nature to stray once in a while, whether out of curiosity or drunkenness or misplaced lust. Besides, I always felt that their marriage was tough enough to withstand a little philandering.

After I'd met Catherine, I told them I had a new girlfriend, and said I had hopes for the relationship, though I didn't go as far as telling them her name. Mike did ask what this one had that the others didn't and, of course, I couldn't say that she had a perfect pair of feet. I simply said she was American, and that seemed enough of an explanation for them. Natasha said I should bring her over but we all knew that I wouldn't.

Natasha was, no doubt, a very attractive woman. She was big hipped and big breasted, though her figure was more earth mother than hour glass. I don't imagine she had to fight men off, but I'm sure she must have had her opportunities. For the record, her feet were nicely arched, but much too plump and short-toed for my tastes. Consequently I entertained no feelings of lust for her whatsoever. I didn't want anything like that from her. At the time I thought that was just as well, and subsequent events would prove that I was absolutely right to think that.

Eight

In one sense, what I wanted from Catherine was entirely simple and straightforward. I simply wanted her to make her feet available to me and I would do the rest. I would be the active partner, the one in need and yet the giver. I would treat her feet well, pamper them, adore them, dress them up in beautiful shoes, just the way any lover would treat any object of desire. And, even though Catherine's feet would be the primary sexual focus, I wouldn't be totally selfish. I wouldn't neglect the rest of her. I'd do my damndest to satisfy her in all the more usual ways as well. The standard components of a good conventional relationship would not be entirely absent. I had every intention of being thoughtful, considerate and generous. I would try not to be too demanding, nor too jealous.

But inevitably it would not be a strictly conventional relationship. Mine was not the kind of love that led to domesticity, joint home-ownership, marriage, babies and all that stuff. It didn't lead to sharing a social life, to meeting friends and relatives. In fact I found it hard to imagine what it *did* lead to. I couldn't quite envisage how our future lives might shape themselves around each other. Nevertheless, fragile and provisional though our relationship was, I envisaged that we would in some sense continue.

I suppose I imagined that we would go on leading our quotidian lives as we always had, though I had no idea what that involved for Catherine, and occasionally we would come together, at her place or mine (although so far she had refused to come to my home), or perhaps in some hotel or some risky semi-public place where we would drink, talk briefly, then have intense, fetishistic sex. The meeting in the wine bar when I masturbated into her shoe was only the first of several such encounters.

Faithfulness certainly didn't seem to be important. I felt it wouldn't have bothered me if Catherine had been involved with, or committed to, any number of other people, just so long as she continued to see me, continued to let me love her feet. I eventually realized I was quite wrong to think that, but this discovery was some way off.

As for what Catherine wanted, that was a mystery. She had not sought out a fetishist. I had simply turned up and presented myself to her. I had always imagined there might be a woman out there who was my sexual mirror-image, someone with perfect feet who was looking for a man who would adore them for her. Even though Catherine enjoyed being the object of my obsession she was not precisely that mirror-image. There was always a certain ambivalence, a certain hesitation. She obviously found my fetishism strange and unsettling, but she was ultimately not repelled by it. And her reluctance was not insuperable. Although she hesitated, although she would say she didn't know what she was doing with me, a moment always came when she would give herself over to the perversity of the situation and, as she had shown in the wine bar, as she showed elsewhere, she would respond intensely.

On one of our first 'dates' we went along to a beauty salon and Catherine had a professional pedicure. I was there as an interested (not to say fascinated, not to say fixated) observer. The salon had some aspirations to style and modernity, though it was something of a period piece; lots of mirrors, black sinks, spotlights and networks of chrome railings that had no obvious function.

We met 'our' pedicurist, a young, cheerful, freckled, sturdy-looking girl not more than eighteen years old. Her badge said she was called Sophie. I saw that she was wearing some flat, open-toed sandals which weren't at all appealing, yet the feet within them looked nice enough. The toes were good and straight, and the nails though unpainted were shapely and glossy. I was encouraged.

There were only a couple of women in the salon having their hair done, having facials and manicures, so it wasn't crowded. Nevertheless it seemed like an all too public space. I wanted Catherine's pedicure to be done in private and I was pleased when we were escorted away from the main area of the salon into a special pedicure section. Catherine sat down in a raised hydraulic chair, not unlike a dentist's, although it was upholstered in white leatherette. There was a footstool and a low table from which Sophie was going to operate.

'When did you last have a pedicure?' she asked.

'It's my first time,' said Catherine.

Sophie nodded knowingly, and said, 'Basically we recommend a pedicure and paraffin treatment every three weeks.'

'Paraffin?' Catherine asked.

'Oh yes,' Sophie confirmed, though without explaining anything.

She began laying out her instruments, the tools of her trade: toenail clippers, toe separators, pumice stone, different grades of emery board, cotton-wool swabs, and then a variety of bottles, one or two that were labelled as nail-varnish removers or cuticle softeners, but mostly blank and inscrutable. Then she produced an enamel bowl full of water and set it at Catherine's feet.

'Now there's nothing in here to worry about,' she said. 'Just water, Epsom salts, plus a few drops of essential oils: lavender, rosemary and geranium. And I want you to give your feet a really good soak.'

Catherine did as she was told, and our pedicurist then disappeared. I'm sure there's nothing inherently pleasurable about sitting in a salon soaking your feet in lukewarm water. In fact, if Catherine was anything to go by, it's a procedure that's likely to bring on a fit of the giggles. I didn't giggle but I would have agreed that the pedicure had started on a moderately absurd note. After fifteen minutes we were thinking we might have been forgotten, but Sophie returned, bouncy as a puppy, carrying a big absorbent towel with which she dried Catherine's feet.

'Now I'm going to put on some avocado foot cream,' she said. 'That will soothe your soles nicely and improve circulation.'

We nodded and watched as she worked some greenish goo into Catherine's feet.

'You know,' said Sophie, 'a lot of people think that walking around barefoot is good for you, but I disagree. You're all too likely to cut your feet or pick up a fungus or bacteria. And, of course, you must always wear plastic or rubber sandals at the health club or in poolside showers.'

We both assured her that we would.

'Next, I usually have to remove any old or chipped nail varnish. Not a pleasant job, and obviously not necessary in this case, and then I cut and shape the nails. Now you'd think that's a simple enough procedure, but you'd be amazed how easy it is to get wrong, and badly cut toe-nails can be really dangerous.'

'Really?' said Catherine, all exaggerated awe.

'Really. Because badly cut toe-nails affect the way you walk, they cause discomfort and that can cause you to transfer too much weight to the heels. There's really only one option here. I'm going to cut them straight across, anything else can give you ingrown toenails. And length is all important too, short enough so that they don't touch the edges of your shoes or cut into adjacent toes, but long enough so that they provide some protection to the tips of your toes. Is that clear?'

She looked at both of us, willing us to understand, as though she had explained, albeit in layman's terms, some state-of-the-art piece of microsurgery. We confirmed that we understood.

She began to work with her clippers, purposefully but delicately. It seemed to me she was performing an intensely, unbearably intimate task. Much as I loved Catherine's feet, I wasn't sure that I'd have been able to clip her toenails in that way. Something about it would have felt too intrusive. Sophie had no such qualms. Soon she put down the clippers and worked on the nails using a smoothing disc and a buffer.

Next she pushed back what little cuticle there was round the edges of the nails, and she looked at Catherine's feet in admiration, though I wasn't sure whether it was in admiration of the feet themselves or of her own work. She felt Catherine's heels and the balls of her feet.

'Normally I'd now have a go with a skin slougher or pumice to remove any dead skin or calluses, but there's no need for that here,' she said. 'You've got really good feet. Really.'

Then it was time to varnish the nails. You know it was Cecil Beaton who said of Coco Chanel, 'She wore no red

56

on her fingernails but reddened the tips of her toes on the theory that feet were a dreary business and required every aid.' Ever since I read that I've felt very differently about Coco Chanel. Dreary business indeed. Not that Sophie appeared to find the business at all dreary.

'The most popular colour is still the good old fire-engine red,' she said. 'That's because it looks good with almost any kind of skin. Nude colours or corals can be used to enhance a dark or tanned skin tone, and these days we can have a lot of fun with metallics.'

'No,' I said as gently as I could, not wanting to disappoint her. 'I don't think we want to have fun with metallics.'

'Are you sure? I can recommend Revlon's Sahara Gold, from their Exotica collection, which personally I'd describe as giving a shimmering, crystalline, golden-brown effect.'

'No,' I said.

'Or Silver Sparkle by Creative Nail Design.'

'No,' said Catherine, helping me out. 'We'll go for the good old fire-engine red.'

'I think you've made a very good choice,' said Sophie.

She inserted foam rubber separators between Catherine's toes and applied a base coat to the nails, and when it was dry she started to put on the red varnish. She had the steadiest, most precise hand I think I've ever seen. Each nail was painted in three sure, clean strokes, one down the centre of the nail, then one down each side. There were no blots, no runs, no hint of hesitation. The job was done rapidly, though not hurriedly, and then she allowed five more minutes to pass before applying a clear top coat.

'Now, I want you to sit there and not move a muscle for the next fifteen minutes.'

Catherine did as she was told and Sophie went away again. Catherine's toes were still splayed apart by the separators and they gave her feet a curiously deformed look. But I knew it was going to be worth it. Our pedicurist hadn't really done much that Catherine couldn't have done for herself, yet there was something oddly pleasing about the presence of an outsider, of a professional touch. Whether there was any erotic element to it I wasn't sure.

When the fifteen minutes was up Sophie returned to tell us that the procedure was over.

'Before you go,' she said, 'can I recommend a product called Adiol?'

I'd never heard of it and assumed it was some fancy cosmetic product that she was selling on commission, but no.

'It comes originally from the horse-racing fraternity,' she said. 'Grooms used to apply Adiol to horses' hoofs to strengthen them, but then the grooms themselves noticed their own nails becoming much healthier and stronger.

'You know, nails are structurally very similar to horses' hoofs. So the scientists at Adiol refined their product and Adiol Nail-Strengthening Cream was born. It's rich in vitamin E and collagen but it contains no formaldehyde or toluene, and I can personally vouch for it.'

We were sold, and we bought a bottle. It was time to go home. With some reluctance Catherine slipped on her shoes. It seemed a shame to cover up all that hard pedicuring.

As I was paying Sophie her fee I said, 'Yours is a strange calling, isn't it?'

'What?'

'A strange job, handling people's feet all day.'

She looked mildly offended. I knew I'd said the wrong thing and tried to laugh it off.

'Well, I guess it's not strange at all,' I said. 'There are

probably people who'd pay good money to handle other people's feet all day.'

That was wrong too. She looked at me with what seemed to be practised contempt, as though she had seen right through me and spotted me as just another sicko loser of the sort that she had to deal with all too often.

'It's just a job, all right?'

I said all right, gave her a bigger tip than I might have otherwise, and I hustled Catherine out of the salon.

Catherine and I didn't spend that night together, and alone in my bed, somewhere between waking and sleeping, I had a little sexual fantasy about what might have happened in the salon with Sophie and Catherine. It involved troilism and footsucking and was, I suppose, not really very original. But what was interesting was the way the fantasy had come unbidden. It wasn't as if my sex life with Catherine needed any spicing up. Rather I felt it was an indication that with Catherine anything, any sexual antic or adventure, seemed possible, in fact seemed very likely.

Catherine and I continued to see each other, not too often, perhaps not as often as I would have liked, but continue we did. I wanted her to come to my place, to see the archive if nothing else, but she said she wasn't ready for that yet. So we met in bars, where she would reiterate that she didn't know what she was doing with me, and then we would go back to her place, where what she was doing with me became perfectly clear. Other times we went shopping for shoes.

We were in the shoe department of a big London department store; very smart, moderately exclusive, very expensive. Some of the shoes were arranged on racks, with the more exotic specimens on pedestals or wall-mounted on glass shelves. The department was busy and assistants hard to find, not that we needed any assistance. It was easy enough to take shoes from the displays and try them on, and Catherine did so, to my obvious pleasure, but we were not there to do anything as wholesome and uncomplicated as shopping.

We browsed through the whole department, looking for something very special, the right shoe for the right occasion, and at last we found the one that satisfied our needs. I handed Catherine a single, high-heeled, lizard-skin court shoe. The skin was soft and had a matt finish. It was elegant, narrow and had a long, pointed toe. She took it from me and admired it, then looked around to make sure nobody else was watching. She was wearing a calf-length, wrap-around skirt, with a slit up the side that showed a length of leg as she walked. She was wearing nothing underneath, and she slid the shoe inside the folds of the skirt.

This might have been interpreted as the act of a shoplifter, but that was not what we had in mind at all. Catherine carefully pressed the shoe against her cunt. She exerted a slow, steady, twisting pressure, so that the toe of the shoe parted her and bluntly entered. I watched intently, my gaze partly on what Catherine was doing beneath the skirt, partly on her face, which she was desperately trying to keep impassive.

She had soon done as much as she could with the shoe. She bought it out from beneath the skirt, and handed it back to me. I looked at it and smiled appreciatively when I saw that the toe of the shoe was smeared with her juices. For a second I considered licking them off, but that was not part of the plan. I steadied myself and returned the shoe to its place on the display stand. We moved away, pretended we were still looking round the department, but our attention remained firmly on the lizard skin shoe. We did not have long to wait before someone else tried it on.

She was young, very dark, her body and face very angular. She was sullen but sensual, and she was with her bored, much older husband who watched impatiently as she sat down, shucked off her own footwear and slipped her foot into the lizard-skin shoe. It went on easily and appeared to be a good fit. She extended her leg, held out the foot, turned her ankle so she could see the effect from different angles. She seemed satisfied, though she remained sullen, and she asked an assistant for the other half of the pair. While she was waiting for the assistant to return, something about the shoe caught her attention. She peered at it, and saw there was a mark on the toe, but she didn't know what it was, how could she? She must have thought it was a scuff or a line of dust. She touched the shoe, as though to polish it, and her long, white index finger found itself skimming through the traces from Catherine's vagina and removing them. She looked at the shoe again, seemed pleased. She still didn't know what she had touched.

The assistant returned, the woman tried on the other shoe, declared herself content and her husband paid for them. While she was waiting for the transaction to be completed she absent-mindedly stroked the corner of her mouth with the same finger that had touched the shoe and Catherine's juices.

Later, in Catherine's flat, as we had sex, Catherine's legs up, her feet pressed to my face, I knew we were both thinking about the dark, angular woman in the store. We wondered what she and her husband were doing tonight, whether they were enjoying the reality of the shoes they'd bought as much as we were enjoying the mere thought of them.

Nine

The story of Cinderella is a primary myth for all foot and shoe fetishists, but there are a lot of problems that go with it. At its simplest level, and even to the most unideological observer, it must seem to be peddling some unpleasant nonsense about class and romantic love. The idea that a woman might change her life utterly and for the better simply by dressing up in finery and attending a ball so that she can become a prince's object of desire, is one that we find as suspect as we do improbable. But, of course, it's the glass slipper that really interests me.

How does the slipper come to be so crucial in the story? The prince, let's remember, has spent a certain amount of time with Cinderella. He's talked to her, heard her voice, seen her face, has surely had time enough to gain some sense of her personality. Yet when he begins his search for her, such attributes as personality, face and voice are wholly ignored. He is simply searching for the owner of a certain foot, a foot that will fit the glass slipper she left behind.

It is well known that in Perrault's original French fairytale the slipper is made of fur not glass. Now, there's no shortage of sexual overtones in a fur slipper. Pubic hair is invoked, the interaction of human and animal skin is suggested, and the penetration of a fur opening by a woman's foot is certainly ripe with perverse symbolism. But the plot of *Cinder-*

ella revolves around the slipper fitting only one woman, and the fact is that fur is soft, yielding and could be stretched to fit any number of differently sized feet. A glass slipper, being rigid, has a far more specific fit, and is far less accommodating than fur.

However, if we accept that the slipper is being used as some kind of vaginal symbol, a fur one is surely more serviceable than a glass one. Glass is brittle. It breaks. It is potentially dangerous. One could so easily smash the vessel and cut oneself.

The role of the slipper is made even more complex and perverse, because it's the prince who's the possessor of this symbolic vagina. It belonged to Cinderella but she has run from it, left it behind. When the prince begins his search it's the women of the kingdom who must perform an act of penetration, who must insert their foot into this fragile glass opening that he carries with him.

This is a highly unusual and unlikely way of talking about heterosexual intercourse. The prince is active in his search for the foot, but entirely passive at the moment of insertion. We might easily convince ourselves that the prince is, in some sense, searching for a phallus, but, if so, it's interesting that he's in search of a small, delicate one.

The behaviour of the ugly sisters contains all manner of weirdness too. They know that their feet are too big and ugly for the glass slipper, and, in a later version of the story, they actually have parts of their feet amputated so that they'll be small enough to fit into it. In one case it's the heel, in the other, more alarmingly, it's the big toe. Taken simply as an act of self-mutilation this is shocking enough, but if we allow the foot to be considered as a phallic substitute, the idea becomes one of hysterical violence. Not that the prince is fooled. Cosmetic surgery is no good. The foot must conform to specific criteria but it has to be that way *naturally*.

But does the whole business of the glass slipper work anyway? It is possible that there is something going on here that we could call poetic licence, but we might just as easily call it a clumsy plot device. And given that glass is an improvement on fur, surely it's not credible that a shoe, even when made of glass, however carefully fashioned, however specific to the wearer, would really only fit one woman in the whole kingdom.

Yes, everyone's feet are unique, and if the prince, for example, had taken a Polaroid of Cinderella's feet and gone round the kingdom in search of feet that matched the photograph, then he might well have tracked down Cinderella. But he was just relying on size and shape. How many shoe sizes are there? How many width fittings? How many defining features? Not many. It's hard to imagine a foot so singular that a shoe could be fashioned that would fit this foot and no other.

And here it seems to me the glass slipper functions in yet another way. Glass is transparent. When the glass slipper is on Cinderella's foot, the foot, by definition, remains entirely visible. The foot is contained, restrained, reshaped by the slipper, possibly a little squashed and pushed around, yet every feature can still be seen.

But let's think about Cinderella's feet. She is forced to be a drudge. In English pantomime she is usually to be found barefoot in the kitchen, by the fireplace. And her main job, of course, is to sweep up cinders. However delicate and small and special those feet of hers may be, they will not be clean. They would have been made dirty by treading in ash and coal dust. During the fairy godmother's transformation it is possible to suppose they were made clean by the

64

power of magic, but by the time the prince arrives they would certainly be dirty again.

The prince holds out the delicate glass slipper and Cinderella places her perfect but soiled foot inside it. The long sought fit is achieved. The prince sees the object of his desire encased in glass like a museum specimen. The sullied sexual object is made safe, put behind glass. The prince can see its every detail, but he doesn't need to touch it, indeed he doesn't want to. It is as though the foot is varnished, set in colourless amber. However much he loves it, he won't get his hands or anything else dirty. The man is obviously a fool.

All this Cinderella business was brought into idiosyncratic focus the day I first met Harold Wilmer and had my life changed. Harold was a small, trim, compact man. He must have been sixty years old and yet he was as slight and as lean as a teenager. His face was thin, though hardly wrinkled, and he looked as though he would scarcely ever need to shave. He had the air of a man who might once have been seriously ill. The illness was cured but it had left him brittle. You would not have mistaken him for a happy man, but it seemed to me that he was touched with melancholy, not misery.

His hair was threadbare and his eyes were tired, but he was dapper and alert, and he sat at his workbench wearing a tie and tweed waistcoat under his stained apron. He might have been mistaken for a jeweller or a taxidermist, and I suppose his work had something in common with both those trades, but in fact he was a bespoke shoemaker.

I know a little about shoemaking; not enough to be able to make a shoe, probably not even enough to give instructions to a shoemaker, but I like to think I have enough knowledge of the techniques of shoemaking to be able to appreciate other people's mastery of those techniques. I know that shoemaking is not what it was, that it's become a dying art. Automation and synthetic fabrics have made a lot of the old skills superfluous. Good shoemakers are a rare breed and in danger of extinction.

I know roughly how a shoe should be constructed. First a pattern is made, and this pattern is then cut from the sheet of leather or fabric. This is a highly skilled job and needs to be in tune with the grain and thickness of the material. Once cut, the various upper parts are stitched together, then moulded on a last and brought together with the insole. The sole and heel are then attached, the sock lining inserted and the shoe can come off the last for finishing, i.e. waterproofing, polishing, decorating. That at least is what I'd read in the textbooks. My knowledge was anything but practical.

I have always enjoyed the language of shoemaking. It seems strange and dark and contradictory. For example, the way a shoe is 'lasted' then 'finished'. The man who cuts up the skins is known as the 'clicker'. And much of the vocabulary seems potent and mysterious; words like the 'welt', the 'shank', the 'vamp'.

My knowledge was very useful when I first met Harold. It stopped him thinking I was a fool or a time-waster. I had been aware of his shop long before I was aware of him. I sometimes walked past it on my way to work. It was a small, old-fashioned, bay-fronted establishment, the window always full of clutter: lasts, brushes, shoe-expanders, shoe trees, bottles and tins of leather oil, liquid wax, hide food, dubbin, and a kind of polish called Parade Gloss. His name and his trade, 'bespoke shoemaker', were painted on the glass in gold leaf.

Since he made shoes individually and to order there was

never an array of stock in the window, but occasionally a pair of elegantly constructed brogues or riding boots would make a brief appearance while waiting to be collected. This was not the kind of shoemaking I was interested in. I was scarcely even aware that he made shoes for women at all, but then one day I was walking past his window and saw the most extraordinary pair of women's shoes.

The heels were long and slender, tapering almost to a point, and were made of some kind of burnished red metal. The shoes had peep-toes, the opening more or less semi-circular, the edge of that opening, and the edge of the shoe's mouth, again braided with the same red metal. The body of the shoe was made out of some supremely soft inky black leather, but a tracery of thin red-metal filaments ran across it, less regular than a spider's web, more like spilled wax. The back of the shoe was high and from it emerged two strands of leather, one red, one black, to be tied together as an ankle strap.

Everything about the shoes was remarkable – the extravagance, the richness of the shape and materials – and, even seen through the window, the workmanship was obviously exquisite. They looked totally, indecently out of place, these fierce but wholly feminine objects set amidst the dusty clutter of the rest of the window display. I certainly wanted to buy them for Catherine, but I think it was curiosity as much as anything else that made me enter the shop. How did such outlandish objects come to be here? Who had made them? How was it I had never come across them before?'

I went into the shop and that was when I met Harold Wilmer for the first time. A counter confronted you as soon as you entered, and a long way back in the rear of the premises was a workshop. Here Harold was to be seen sitting at a small workbench, cutting out pieces of leather. He looked up quickly when he saw me and immediately stopped what he was doing, but it took a long time for him to stand up and come to the counter. Even when he arrived he didn't say anything or ask me what I wanted, but he stared at me hard.

I said, 'I'm interested in those shoes in the window.' Still nothing from him, so I said, 'The red and black ones. The women's shoes. For my girlfriend. I was wondering what size they were. How much they cost.'

I don't know why I spoke so hesitantly. I had bought women's shoes often enough before. Harold still didn't say anything but he ambled over to the shop window and with a lot of effort carefully extracted the shoes. He handled them roughly but with affection and held them out so I could look at them.

There was nothing soft or boyish about Harold's hands. They were dark and gnarled, as stained and tanned as some of the leather he worked with. They were an old man's hands and decades of work had made them strong and specialized. The grain stood out, revealing a pattern of small scars, gashes, crescents, healed flaps of skin where knives had slipped and cut into his flesh. And yet they had delicacy, were obviously capable of intricate, detailed work.

I looked at the shoes more carefully. Up close the standard of workmanship was even more extraordinary. I reached out to take them from him, but he held them back. They were for my eyes only. They looked as though they were more or less the right size to fit Catherine, and even if they hadn't been, they would still have been exquisite examples to own, have around and include in the archive. I peered inside to see whether they had a size. They didn't, but they did have the maker's mark, one I had seen before; the outline of a footprint with a lightning flash at its centre.

'I'll take them,' I said.

Harold ignored me and replied, 'I don't feel absolutely comfortable about selling them, you know.'

'No?'

'I made them for a client, a long-standing client. Unfortunately she doesn't have any use for them now. She died before I could finish them.'

'I'm sorry to hear that,' I said automatically.

'I don't see why. The sorrow is all mine. It was a pleasure to make shoes for her. More than a pleasure.'

The mention of his dead client had pitched him into a sudden and profound depression. I really didn't need this. I just wanted to buy the shoes. I didn't even much care what the price was. I certainly didn't want to get involved with some stranger's personal tragedy. I did my best to change the subject. I said, 'I've been past your shop before, but I never realized you made women's shoes.'

'Ladies, women,' he said. 'I don't care so long as they're appreciative.'

He looked down at the shoes he was holding, then at me.

'I know it sounds absurd,' he said, 'but I'd like to be sure these shoes will be going to a good home.'

This was crazy. What did he want from me? It's no easy business to convince someone that you are a worthy possessor of their handmade shoes, and I wasn't keen to try. On the other hand I did want to make the purchase. All I could say was, 'I think my girlfriend would be very appreciative indeed.'

He looked at me even more closely, as though by examining me he would be able to learn what kind of woman I might be involved with.

'Come on,' I said. 'They were in the window. Let's do business. How much do you want for them?'

'It's not a question of money,' he said.

Oh, Jesus, I thought to myself, what does he want me to do? Undergo an initiation rite?

'I'm not selling these shoes because I need the cash,' he said. 'In fact, I'm tempted to keep them. But I happen to believe that a shoe needs to function before I can consider it a success. Shoes have to be worn before they can live. I want my shoes to live.'

I nodded. What he said made perfect sense to me. It was a sentiment I shared, but I didn't want to agree too readily in case he thought I was trying to con him into parting with the shoes.

He said, 'I wouldn't want you to buy them blind. You bring your young lady in and let her try them on. We'll see if they're a fit.'

I realized he was talking about something far more subtle and complex than the matter of foot size. It seemed to me that he wanted to be sure that Catherine fitted the shoes rather than vice versa. It occurred to me to tell him that Catherine already owned a pair of his shoes, but I resisted on the grounds that he might well be insulted to learn that his work had turned up in a second-hand clothes shop in Islington. However, I didn't have the slightest doubt that Catherine would measure up to any standard he cared to set. Whether she would want to participate in this charade was another matter altogether.

She took some persuading. She didn't want to play games with some cranky old shoemaker. Furthermore she said, reasonably enough, the chances of the shoes fitting her were remote. Who did I think she was? Cinderella? And, even if they *did* fit, she wasn't sure she wanted to wear a dead woman's shoes. She said she might not like the shoes, but I assured her there wasn't the slightest chance of that. What actually clinched it was telling her that the shoes contained the same trade mark as her zebra-skin ones. Those shoes, she said, were the sexiest, best-fitting shoes she'd ever owned. Finally, though still a little warily, she agreed to come with me.

A couple of days later we went to the shop. The shoes were not in the window and I wondered at first whether we'd waited too long, whether some more persuasive customer had beaten us to it and talked Harold into selling them. We entered the shop. Harold looked up, saw us, and said, perhaps sarcastically, 'Ah, my latest customers.'

I introduced Catherine. He looked her up and down. It was not prurient, not even sexual, and yet his gaze seemed to strip her bare of everything but essentials. He motioned for her to come in behind the counter, into his work area, and to sit down on a blue velvet banquette that was installed there. The moment she was seated he squatted at her feet and removed the shoes she was wearing, strappy sandals, nothing too extreme. He took her bare feet in his old dark hands and touched them carefully. Again there was nothing lascivious in his manner and yet it was an act of great intimacy. Harold's gnarled, scarred fingers squeezed, stroked and examined Catherine's feet. He traced the paths of veins and muscles, bent the toes back and forth gently so he could see the way they moved and functioned. He didn't smile or look pleased. It was too serious a matter for that. He appeared professional, disinterested, but at last he nodded to himself in satisfaction.

He went to a locker, opened it, got out the red and black shoes and brought them for Catherine. I could tell immediately that she liked them. Harold slipped the shoes on to her feet. Her pale skin lay in stark contrast to the soft, dark leather and the metal tracery. Most important, the shoes fitted perfectly, absolutely perfectly. They could have been made for her. At the time that didn't seem so strange; I knew that, unlike Cinderella's glass slipper, there were any number of women whose feet these shoes would have fitted.

Catherine stood up and paced across the workshop while Harold and I watched intently, though with our different forms of fascination. I was looking through the eyes of a lover. He, I thought, was looking through the eyes of a craftsman. But we were both delighted, as was Catherine. She said she loved both the look and the feel. She went back and forth a few more times, her walk becoming a feline, predatory stalk. Then she smiled at Harold and, in his ancient, boyish, uncertain way, he smiled back.

'They're something special,' she said.

Harold nodded in agreement. He was pleased that she liked them, but I got the feeling it was she who was being judged not the shoes. Harold did not need anyone else's opinion to confirm the worth of what he had made.

'You can have the shoes,' he said, and Catherine and I responded enthusiastically. We had passed the test and been found worthy: a slightly absurd test it seemed, but at least we could now pay, take the shoes and go.

'How much?' I asked.

'They're my present to you,' Harold said. 'My gift.'

I said, hold on, I couldn't possibly accept them for free. That was partly because I didn't want to take advantage of the old man, but more importantly because I didn't want to feel beholden to him. But he wasn't having any of it.

He said, 'I put those shoes in the window hoping that they'd attract the right sort of customer. And they have.

You're here. They're yours. I'm delighted. But there's one condition.'

'No,' I said. 'No conditions. Let's keep this businesslike. Let me give you some money.'

Ignoring me he turned to Catherine and said, 'The condition is that you let me continue to make shoes for you.'

'What kind of shoes?' she asked.

'Any shoes I like. Anything and everything I want. I don't think you'll be disappointed. And I wouldn't charge you for those shoes either.'

I looked at Catherine. Given her reluctance to come to the shop in the first place, I assumed she'd find the idea of 'conditions' as objectionable as I did. But she was now strutting around the place, modelling the shoes, looking and behaving like a sex queen, a smile of utter, indecent pleasure plastered across her face. There was no doubt that she'd agree.

'Harold,' she said. 'This could be the start of something big.'

When we got back to Catherine's flat, we took the shoes out of their tissue-lined box and set them on a glass table in the middle of the living room. Normally I would have had the immediate desire to christen a pair of newly acquired shoes, to use them as an essential part of some sexual act or performance. But these shoes from Harold Wilmer produced a curious sort of inaction, a stasis. You had to pause, stop dead, and admire them.

'They're some shoes,' said Catherine.

'They are,' I agreed.

'It's a pity Harold's so creepy.'

'Yes, he is a bit creepy, isn't he?' I said.

'I wonder who he made the shoes for. Who she was. What happened to her? How did she die?'

'I wonder what happened to the rest of her shoes.'

'It's a pity you're so creepy too,' she said.

She was making a joke, but a part of her obviously meant it.

'I thought my creepiness was what attracted you to me,' I said.

She didn't have a ready answer for that.

'I guess we needn't ever go back to Harold's shop,' she said after a while. 'I mean we have the shoes, right?'

'That wouldn't be fair,' I said.

'I guess not,' she said. 'A deal's a deal. Besides, he does make amazing shoes. Where else are we going to get more shoes like this? For free.'

I frowned. That part of the bargain was still worrying me.

'I don't like to get something for nothing,' I said. 'There's no such thing. We'll have to find a way of paying him. If he won't take money we'll have to give him something else. Food hampers or sweaters or whatever else he does for kicks.'

'Are you sure he does anything for kicks?'

'Everybody does something,' I replied.

Catherine seemed to be considering this proposition but then a new thought struck her.

'Hey,' she said, 'when we stop seeing each other, who gets custody of the shoes? You or me?'

'I don't know,' I said. 'Maybe we could not stop seeing each other.'

'No,' she said. 'I suspect that isn't an option.'

Ten

And so our relationship with Harold began in earnest. A few days later we returned to the shop and he began the process of fitting. He measured Catherine's feet, made drawings and diagrams, jotted pages of notes to himself. That much was as expected, but then he said, 'Now I need to make a cast.'

'A cast?'

'Yes, a sort of life mask of the young lady's feet.'

'You mean like a plaster cast?' Catherine asked.

'Yes. It's not absolutely essential to the shoemaking process, but a cast reveals all sorts of details about the foot that are invisible to the naked eye. It enables me to create a more perfect fit.'

There's a famous photograph of Ferragamo surrounded by his lasts. They represent the feet of his famous clients and are marked with their names: Claudette Colbert, Greta Garbo, Sophia Loren. The lasts are made of wood and although they obviously depict the size and the shape of the foot very accurately, they don't show any detail, no bone structure or veins, not even the toes. I could see that a 'life mask' would be a much more faithful replica, even though I wasn't sure how necessary that detail would be when it came to making shoes.

Harold continued, 'I'll need to make a mould using the sort of bandage they use to set broken limbs. Once I've got the mould I can use it to make perfect models of the feet. I tend to use plaster but you could use lots of different things. I could just as easily make models in wax or plasticine, even jelly.'

The prospect of having Catherine's feet cast in jelly was a bizarre one. What flavour would I choose? Strawberry? Lime? Calves-foot? Incidentally, there are a couple of Aboriginal tribes in south-eastern Australia who used to eat the feet of their slain enemies; but I'm rambling.

Harold began to make the cast. I thought it would be a difficult and painstaking process, but Harold went about it in a perfectly matter of fact way. He began by coating Catherine's feet in Vaseline, which he described as 'the releasing agent'. I watched his hands smearing the stuff all over Catherine's bare feet, his short, dark fingers swirling over every part of them, smoothing them down, burrowing in between the toes. Harold retained an entirely formal air while completing his task, but for me there was something utterly profane about it.

Then he asked Catherine to arch her feet as though she was on tiptoe or, I suppose, as though she was wearing high heels. He then wrapped the feet in the medical bandages he'd spoken of and slapped white liquid plaster over them. We had to wait for them to set, and Catherine was commanded not to move, but the whole business was brief and painless. Harold was soon cutting the set bandage and releasing Catherine's feet. It took less time and was far less intimidating than the pedicure had been.

Harold said he didn't need us any more. He said that now he had the moulds he could make the actual casts in our absence. In fact, as Catherine pointed out after we'd left the shop, he could make any number of them, in a wide variety of media, and who knows to what uses he might put them. She giggled. The thought didn't displease her.

Before long a pair of plaster casts duly arrived for me in the post. They were meticulously packed and I undid the parcel with a kind of awe. Harold had been perfectly correct. I thought I knew every nook and crevice of Catherine's feet, and yet seeing them this way, inert and perfectly white, revealed new features, small indentations and elevations that I had not noticed so clearly before. I was looking at a new map, a new geography. The effect was strangely hyper-real, as though the replicas contained more information, more detail than the feet themselves.

I handled them for a long time, held them up to the light, placed them in various locations in my living room and bedroom to discover where they could be seen to their best advantage. They weren't, of course, as appealing as the real thing, as Catherine's real flesh, but as fetish objects they were more exciting than the majority of feet I had ever encountered.

Harold wasn't very explicit about what he would do with the casts. The shoes weren't going to be constructed around the plaster, he was making wooden lasts for that. Rather it seemed as though he wanted to have these models of Catherine's feet in front of him as he designed and made a new pair of shoes, as a reminder of Catherine and as an inspiration.

Catherine and I still had no idea what kind of shoes Harold was going to come up with. We had both asked what he had in mind but he told us we would have to wait and see. He said it as though we were over-inquisitive children, and I think he took some pleasure in teasing us, in denying us gratification, and yet there was nothing frivolous in his approach to his craft.

I asked if he had any other shoes he could show us, some

77

earlier examples of his work, but he said that all his shoes were now with their rightful owners. Didn't he at least keep a few photographs or working drawings, I asked. Surely they'd have been good for drumming up business if nothing else. But Harold said he kept nothing. Once the shoes had been made he was finished with them. They had a life of their own, they went out into the world. He might occasionally see them in action, being worn by their owners, but at that point he was just a spectator, they were no longer his, he had no claim on them. As a confirmed archivist I found this detachment very peculiar, but I didn't doubt that Harold was telling the truth.

Making this new pair of shoes for Catherine was a slow and painstaking business, and Harold was not going to be rushed. I knew better than to pester him but the anticipation was killing. I tried to imagine what he might be making but I didn't want to fantasize too much in case my imaginings and expectations became so extreme that reality could never live up to them.

But the day finally arrived when Harold was ready to reveal his creation. We were summoned for eight in the evening and I took along a bottle of champagne, as though it might be a party or the launch of a ship. Harold accepted half a glass and then put it down absent-mindedly. His thoughts were elsewhere. For him there seemed to be a lot riding on this pair of shoes, more than I would have thought reasonable. After much prevarication, and what I took to be false modesty, Harold at last showed us the shoes, and they were truly glorious.

The back, sides, heels, all the basic form were styled like a traditional, if extraordinarily high-heeled, court shoe. They were elegant, classic and made of superbly malleable black kid. But there was nothing traditional about the toes of the shoes. They were made of black and white snakeskin, or, to be more accurate, each shoe had at its apex the head of a real snake, the eyes glassily black, the mouths wide open, fangs visible. But the snake heads weren't mere adornment, they were part of the shoe's structure, and the open jaws formed peep-toes, and when Catherine put the shoes on her lacquered nails were visible in the snake's throat, the red varnish in rich contrast to the black and white diamonds of the snakeskin.

Catherine and I were speechless with admiration. She walked round the workshop in the shoes and it seemed as though she had grown in stature and voluptuousness. Her walk and her figure, her whole body were sensual and provocative, utterly carnal. I wanted to fuck her there and then, and there's no greater compliment to a pair of shoes than that. More to the point, and as I could plainly see, they made Catherine want to be fucked there and then too. We both thanked and congratulated Harold. I toasted him and said he was a master, that these were the most exotic and wonderful shoes I'd ever seen.

'I think we have a major success on our hands, Harold,' Catherine agreed.

But Harold didn't seem to share our enthusiasm. He looked profoundly melancholy. He hadn't touched his champagne.

'They're good shoes,' he said. 'There's nothing wrong with them. A lot of people would be delighted to have made them, but I know they're only a partial success. I have to go back to the drawing board.'

Although I would have preferred Harold to be happy, I didn't read too much into his dissatisfaction. He obviously cared deeply about his work, his standards were sky high, and I thought his sense of failure was only that of the true perfectionist. However sublime a creation might be, and these new shoes seemed utterly sublime to me, their creator might always have a sense that they were flawed and imperfect. That, I supposed, was what kept all artists and craftsmen going, the urge to try again, the desire to perfect the imperfectible. And, let's face it, I was very happy for Harold to keep trying and failing if all his failures were going to be as magnificent as these. I was very happy indeed that he was going to be designing and making more shoes for Catherine.

The snake shoes were great for sex. Catherine and I went home, and on this occasion there was no time for contemplation. I put my tongue inside the snake's mouth to lick Catherine's toes. She would walk round her flat, naked but for the shoes, an act that rapidly led to more bouts of sex. I assumed Harold would be delighted by all this, not that we told him precisely what use we made of his shoes, there seemed no need to, obviously he already knew. What else were his kind of shoes for?

I was aware that this was not the usual relationship that existed between shoe wearer and shoemaker. Given that even the best shoes are often machine made, the wearer seldom has any sense of the maker's identity. In this case we obviously had a precise sense of Harold's personality, and in a strange way Harold Wilmer became a real if distant presence in the sex that Catherine and I had together.

For that reason, among others, over the next few weeks I found myself thinking often about Harold and his work. I knew he was making another pair of shoes for Catherine and although I wondered exactly what he was up to, I no longer had any anxiety about what he would produce. I knew they would be extraordinary and magnificent. It was like looking forward to a surprise party.

When a couple of weeks had passed and I hadn't heard

from him I decided to call in at the shop, not because I wanted to harass him, but because I couldn't contain my curiosity any longer.

The shop was open so I entered. Harold was sitting immobile at his workbench, one hand up to his brow as though he might be shading his eyes from the light, but I could tell that in reality he was weeping. I was embarrassed. I felt I was intruding.

'Is this a bad time?' I asked. 'Shall I come back later?'

He raised his head, looked at me and said, 'It'll be exactly the same later. Now that Ruth's dead I just don't . . .'

'Ruth?' I asked.

'Ruth, the woman I used to make shoes for, the red and black ones that first brought you in here.'

'The one you said was a special customer?'

'Yes. But she was a lot more than that.'

'I'm sorry.'

'Now she's gone, I just don't care about anything very much any more.'

I hoped that wasn't literally true. I hoped he wasn't trying to tell me that he'd stopped caring about his craft, that he wasn't going to make any more shoes. I wasn't selfish enough to ask him that directly, but there seemed no point in trying to be discreet. So I said, 'Tell me about Ruth. Who was she exactly?'

'She was a whore,' Harold replied. 'And I'm not speaking metaphorically. She got paid very well for having sex with strange men. She was very good, I understand, well worth the extra. And I made her shoes for her. She always said she could charge even more when she was wearing shoes I'd made.'

He smiled wryly and I wasn't sure whether or not I ought to smile back.

81

'We weren't attached,' he said. 'We weren't lovers. I never made love to her. That would have spoiled everything, although everything's spoiled anyway.

'I know it's absurd to fall in love with a prostitute. It's a thankless task. It's madness. There's no possible joy in it. The woman you love sells herself to other men. She will tell you that she's only selling her body, but you know it's more complex than that. It really isn't possible for anyone to constantly have sex with unknown men, day after day, night after night, in hotel rooms, in rented flats, in the backs of cars, without losing something vital. I don't know what you'd call that something, but sooner or later it just disappears. It trickles away.

'I got angry with her sometimes but I never tried to change her, never tried to make her stop. There were times when I'd want to hurt someone, her or her clients. But I never did. I just kept on making shoes for her to be fucked in, and the only one who got hurt was me.'

'How did Ruth die?' I asked. I feared the worst: suicide or drugs or Aids, something lurid and dramatic.

'Cancer,' he said. 'Banal, yes?'

'No, not banal,' I said.

'She was the only person in the world I ever needed, the only person who ever needed me.'

'Hey, Harold,' I said. 'Catherine and I need you. We need you to carry on making shoes.'

It was supposed to be something of a joke, an attempt to make him feel needed without sounding too sentimental, and maybe it worked.

'Just before you arrived that first day,' he said, 'I was seriously contemplating suicide. I still think about it. It feels like a real option. But you came into the shop, asked about the shoes, and I thought possibly, just possibly, there might be some point carrying on. And possibly, just possibly there is. So long as I can carry on making shoes, practising my art, having someone like Catherine to wear them, then maybe . . .'

I tried to make light of what he was saying. I'd never wanted to be beholden to Harold Wilmer in the first place; now it looked as though he was trying to make me responsible for whether he lived or died.

Nevertheless, I found myself saying, 'Hey, Harold, you can't commit suicide until you've made Catherine at least another hundred pairs of shoes.'

Harold gave a wispy, resilient little smile and told me to come back in a week with Catherine when he'd have a brand new pair of shoes to show us.

Eleven

There have been times in my life when I've thought of becoming professionally involved with women's feet. I've wondered what it might be like to be a chiropodist, a reflexologist, even, conceivably, a pedicurist.

But chiropody would have been no good because it involves looking at feet that have something wrong with them. There might be some satisfaction in improving them, in making them healthy again, but the daily grind of foot imperfections would have been intolerable.

Reflexology might have been better in that you would encounter a cross-section of feet, and some of these would no doubt be very attractive. But my observations tell me that the percentage of attractive feet in the world is remarkably small, and you'd still have to spend a lot of time feeling the pressure points on a lot of mundane, not to say downright ugly, feet.

A shoe-shop job would certainly have been appealing, especially if you were working in a place that sold really exotic footwear to really glamorous women. But the main problem there (apart from the obvious one that shoe-shop assistants obviously earn a pittance) was that I might like the job too much for my own good. Put me in a situation where I'm crouched on the floor with some gorgeous foot, helping its owner try on some beautiful creation in wonderful, soft red leather with black silk ankle straps and, frankly,

I don't know that I could keep up my professional manner.

All the above problems would apply to being a pedicurist and, besides, I think that most women are sufficiently aware of the intimate and sensual nature of the foot not to be all that keen to have some strange man fiddling around with their toes.

I'm sure that being a shoe designer, or even the right sort of shoemaker, would have fulfilled a lot of my needs. But I never had any talent for it. I'm a connoisseur not a creator, a willing member of the audience, but not a provider of the entertainment.

So I did what I did, this responsible but dull job I've spoken of. I was a manager, I suppose, a financial manager. There were people around me, of more or less equal status, who called themselves planners and analysts. Some called themselves executives. But if anybody outside of work ever asked me what I did for a living, I'd say I worked in an office. That was as much information as anybody needed, and certainly as much as I wanted to give.

I worked with a certain number of women. Some of them were attractive and some of them occasionally (very occasionally) wore FMs. I looked but I didn't touch. I was appreciative but I kept it to myself. I wasn't sure what the consequences would have been of having my colleagues know that I was a foot and shoe fetishist, but I didn't want to find out.

There's a story in Ali MacGraw's autobiography about when she goes to model for Salvador Dali. She walks into his suite at the St Regis Hotel. She's wearing a fake Chanel suit and flattened pearl ear-rings. The room's full of strange ill-matched Spanish furniture, and Mozart is playing on a tiny transistor radio.

Immediately he asks her to take off all her clothes. She's

reluctant, a little scared, but she is a model after all. Dali is a major artist, she would certainly like to be immortalized, and even if the old guy is up to no good she reckons she's young enough and strong enough to fight him off. She strips as requested.

He tells her to sit at one of the tables and he takes his place opposite her. She sits down on a wrought-iron chair, adopts a pose, shoulders back, head up. The metal strips of the chair press into her body. She is very uncomfortable. Dali stares hard at her. Well, yes, that's all right, that's what artists are supposed to do. He picks up a stick of charcoal, rolls it between his fingers and immediately drops it at her feet. She moves as though to pick it up. 'No,' he says. 'Don't move. Hold the pose.'

She does as he tells her. He bends down to pick up the charcoal, goes on all fours, starts crawling around under the table. Poor old devil, she thinks. Then she becomes aware that something very strange is happening. At floor level, under the table where she can't see, Salvador Dali, the great artist, is breathing a little heavily, is making a slurping noise, and is methodically sucking each of her toes in turn.

You see, if I'd been an artist it might all have been all right. Strange fetishistic stuff is fine if you're a genius. It's regarded as par for the course. And there are probably quite a few jobs, arty, trendy, creative, media-type jobs where nobody would bat an eyelid, where a fetish would be regarded as desirable and interesting; but I was never in one of those jobs and I never really wanted to be. Frankly, I was always glad to have a few secrets that I kept from the people I worked with, to have something that was uniquely and covertly mine.

86

Twelve

It is a short step from being a student of one's own life to being its curator; hence my archive. I feel ready to talk about my archive now. Fetishists, I understand, tend to be great accumulators, great keepers of files and samples, photographs and cuttings, and I was no exception. My archive was large and impressive and I did from time to time feel the urge to share it with someone. I can't think of any circumstances in which I'd have brought a man to look at it. It was the sort of place I'd only bring a woman, and even then only the right sort of woman, someone like Catherine, although I knew there was nobody exactly like her.

Let's imagine you were such a woman. Let's imagine I had invited you to my house to see my archive. How would it be? It would be much like this. We would go by taxi to the small terraced house in West London where I live. We would enter the hall and I would probably invite you into the living room and offer you a drink. At first all you'd see would be a bachelor's place, a moderately expensive hi-fi, a cheap colour TV, a few items of chrome and leather furniture that some people would probably consider a bit naff and dated. It would not look like the obvious place for a collection of sexual exotica. It would seem far too mundane and ordinary. You might notice the Allen Jones print on the wall and that would be a clue, but even so it would all seem surprisingly homely. You would be reassured or disappointed depending on your disposition. (Catherine, when I finally persuaded her to come to my house, was taut with nervousness.) I wouldn't try to force you into anything. Only after a drink or two, and only if you were still sure you wanted to press on, would I invite you down to the cellar where the archive was kept.

I would carefully open the group of locks that secures the cellar door. I would turn on the staircase lights, warm but not too bright, and as we descended you'd see more pictures on the walls: a Helmut Newton photograph, that you might recognize from *White Women*, showing a pair of manacled feet in supremely glossy red high heels. You would notice working drawings by shoe designers, some Warhol shoe sketches, and a large medical drawing of a foot blown up from *Gray's Anatomy*.

At the bottom of the stairs we would stand together in a small cluttered workroom or office. You would see the rows of books and magazines all relating to my interest, books like Rétif de la Bretonne's *Contemporaines*, John F. Oliver's *Sexual Hygiene and Pathology*, Rossi's *The Sex Life of the Foot and Shoe* in several editions, magazines like *Heels and Hose*, *Footsie*, *Instep*. You would see filing cabinets bulging with photographs and newspaper clippings, and of course you would see my many, many scrapbooks.

I began making these in very early adolescence. I would look through fashion magazines, occasionally through soft-core pornography. I would see shoes or bare feet that appealed to me and I would cut out the photograph and stick it in my scrapbook. I imagine a lot of boys do that sort of thing. Sometimes I would cut out the entire image to show the woman's face, body and clothes. But all too often I found the face, body and clothes quite unerotic, quite irrelevant and a positive distraction from the shoes and feet. In those cases I would simply cut the woman off at mid-calf. This seemed a harmless enough activity, and it brought with it certain satisfactions. Yet I was aware that I was not master of my own fate. I was relying on the editorial control of the people producing the magazines. I decided to seize the means of production.

Like many men I used to take photographs of my girl-friends; of their faces and bodies, sometimes naked, usually clothed. But I soon became more specific. I began to take pictures just of their feet, resting on a cold stone floor, or on a soft fine rug. Sometimes they would be wearing shoes I had chosen and bought for them, sometimes they would be bare.

I suppose I've always been reasonably 'successful' with women, though it's not a term I like. I had a lot of experience. I had a lot of girlfriends. I soon had quite a collection of photographs of their feet. Some found it odd, but few objected. When I was alone I would often spread out these photographs on my desk, arrange them in patterns, in groupings. They were an aid to memory, a kind of souvenir, but also a kind of harem. But, of course, there are far more women, far more attractive feet in the world than one could ever know or make contact with. And one of the greatest pleasures for someone like me is that one may encounter powerful erotic stimuli in quite casual, quite ordinary contexts in the course of one's daily life. It isn't like that for all fetishists. If you are obsessed with bare buttocks, there is a prescribed and extremely limited number of places where you are likely to encounter them; not in the street, for example, not on public transport, not in every home, at every party, at every nightclub. But these are all places where one finds beautiful feet and shoes.

Inevitably these encounters tend to be short and fleeting. A spectacular pair of FMs walks by you in a crowded street. You experience a sharp pang of excitement, but it is here, then gone. It's true that I have been known to follow a really fine pair of feet, and that can be exciting in itself, but it is ultimately unsatisfactory. I needed some means of making these chance experiences more real and permanent.

I bought a small, leather shoulder-bag and cut a hole in the side large enough to accommodate the lens of a fixed focus, automatic camera. The camera was lined up with the hole, then attached to the inside of the bag, and I ran a cable release from the camera, out of the bag, up through the shoulder strap to my hand. I walked the streets carrying the bag, and when I saw an attractive pair of feet belonging to a woman who was standing at a bus stop or looking in a shop window or waiting for a friend, I would stand beside her as though I was waiting too. Then I would take the bag off and set it down on the ground with the camera lens pointing towards the feet, and I would squeeze the cable release to make a permanent record of the subject.

Results were mixed but not wholly unsuccessful. Sometimes the pictures were blurred, because I had nudged the bag or because the feet had moved, and sometimes someone would walk between us as I was taking the photograph, but, on the whole, I achieved my goal. I captured images of feet and shoes that I would never have been able to possess in any other way. They were a crucial part of the archive. If you liked I would show you these photographs, and also the ones I took when asking women to answer my questionnaire. You could see the completed questionnaires too if you wanted.

We could spend a great deal of time in this part of the archive, but sooner or later you might say that all these things were secondary materials. They were not the thing itself. I wouldn't argue with you. I'd simply say, let's move on.

We would then find ourselves in a small, comfortable, predominantly red room. You would see that each of the walls was hung floor to ceiling with thick burgundy chenille curtains. Light would come from a small overhead chandelier, and at the centre of the room you would see a small but plush loveseat and a footstool. You would see a small sideboard and what looked like a cocktail cabinet, but your eye would rapidly move to a row of glass domes on top of the sideboard, the kind used to cover stuffed birds or animals. Anticipating your interest, I would flick a switch and half a dozen spotlights would shine down on the domes. Instead of creatures, each one would contain a pair of shoes. You would see how special these were; one pair with nine or ten inch high heels, another a pair of open-toed ankle boots, another a pair of antique bar shoes. But you wouldn't have time to inspect them closely because I would already be bringing the rest of the room to life.

I would open the sideboard to reveal massed, orderly rows of shoes. I would walk over to the cocktail cabinet, open its doors and show the illuminated interior, and on the shelves where the bottles and glasses should have been there would be an arrangement of kid court shoes in burgundy and black, purple and aquamarine.

Perhaps I would have the video set up in the room and now I would turn it on to show a series of stills, close-ups of shoes and feet in brilliantly crisp, clear detail.

'Impressed?' I might ask, and if, like Catherine, you half-nodded, half-smiled, I would look back as though to say, 'You've seen nothing yet.'

I would go over to the far wall, take hold of one of the

91

stretches of chenille and pull it back like the tabs of a small stage and I would reveal a walk-in cupboard behind it. This, you would see, was the real thing, the inner sanctum, the secret chamber. I would take you by the hand and suggest you take a much closer look.

You would see shelves from floor to ceiling, and display stands in the centre, all crammed with shoes; an Aladdin's cave, a treasure house, but maybe also a reliquary, and maybe partly a prison cell. The sense of mad accumulation would be glorious and yet there might be something sinister about it. By then you would know my tastes and preferences, so none of it would really surprise you. You would have known what to expect and yet you would still be overwhelmed and impressed by the concentration, the intensity of the collection.

Some of the shoes would be opulent and ornate, others simple and classically elegant, some wholly and only fetishistic. And although each shoe would tend to be sleek and discrete, when put together they would create a diffuse, ragged design; black leather nestling next to cerise satin, blue silk next to black lace. The ankle straps from one pair of sandals would spill over into the mouth of a pair of red silk court shoes. Different kinds of leather pierced or inlaid, or concocted into marquetry. You would see bevelled heels and wedges, a few platform soles, some gold lamé, some parrot feathers, fishtail heels, ruby slippers, needle-toes. All the great names would be represented: Vivier, Ferragamo, Perugia, Schiaparelli, Frizon, Cover Girl, Jimmy Choo, Blahnik. There would even be a glass slipper of sorts, although actually it was made of transparent perspex.

It would all be there before you, a collage, a catalogue of shapes, colours and textures that corresponded to my mind, a collection that utterly revealed my personality. I would glow with pride. I'd tell you this was my great work, that it was me. You would see that putting the shoes together like this had been an act of creation and profound self-definition.

You would be filled with questions. I would explain to you that buying the first couple of pairs in this collection was a very big step for me. I was circumspect to start with. I would only buy through mail order. I bought either from specialist fetish suppliers or from conventional mail-order catalogues. But it took very little time before I had the courage to go into shoe shops and buy there. I would always say that I was buying the shoes as a present, which in a sense was true, and none of the shop assistants ever questioned my motives or indicated that they thought I was doing anything peculiar. The ones who served me could hardly have thought I was buying them to wear myself since my own feet are large, and I always bought shoes in conventional women's sizes. In fact I bought them in a variety of sizes so that as and when I had new women in my life, whatever their foot size, I would have something to fit them.

My collection grew, became substantial. I poured a lot of money into it, though probably less than certain men pour into other hobbies. I'm sure it was no more expensive than sailing, golfing or running a classic sports car. There was, however, something lacking. My collection consisted entirely of brand-new shoes. They were often exquisitely beautiful. The styles and shapes were appealing, but as they lined up on my shelves and in my display cabinets, looking pristine and immaculate, they seemed curiously chaste and mute. It proved what I had always known, that a shoe in itself, however full of erotic potential, only comes to life when placed around a human foot. These shoes that I had so carefully selected were used only in the bedroom during sex. They had never been worn in the street. They lacked female warmth, they lacked that patina and character that comes from being worn.

I changed my hunting grounds. I visited second-hand and antique-clothes shops, market stalls, charity shops, and I added to my collection. The shoes thus obtained showed some slight signs of life and wear. They had been gently creased, moulded to the shape of the owners' feet. Sometimes the inside of the shoes bore an imprint of the feet that had worn them. I found this very exciting. There was considerable pleasure to be had in imagining the previous wearer of the shoes, speculating about her feet, her personality, her sexual preferences. And I wondered how she might feel if she knew that her discarded shoes had become objects of fascination for some man, or that I had passed them on to some new woman who had worn them during sex. But of course it was all speculation, all imagination. I would never meet these previous owners.

And that is when I took the next step, and this I think is the only aspect of my obsession that ever actually made me feel ashamed. It was certainly the only thing I ever did that was even remotely illegal. I began to find ways of stealing the shoes from women's feet. Not quite literally. I didn't leap on women, knock them to the ground and rob them. I never used violence; rather I used a great deal of skill and cunning.

There are certain occasions, certain situations, when women take their shoes off in public. It happens in parks or at the beach, although, in the latter case, women rarely wear very exciting shoes when they're walking on sand or shingle. They also take their shoes off in restaurants or bars, at the theatre or cinema. At parties and dances footsore women frequently kick off their shoes and dance in their bare or stockinged feet.

Again, I suppose my greatest advantage in all this was that I didn't look like the sort of man who would steal women's shoes. What would such a man look like in any case? I would saunter past my 'victim', looking innocent but purposeful, as though I had many things on my mind other than women's shoes. It was surprisingly easy. In parks the women would be sunbathing with their eyes closed, or engrossed in a book or listening to a personal stereo. In restaurants and bars they tended to be engrossed in food, drink and conversation. In the theatre or cinema they were watching the entertainment, although the seating arrangements here often made access very difficult. At parties and dances the women were partying or dancing. In none of these situations were they expecting to have their shoes stolen. They would be guarding their handbags, their keys, their credit cards, but they would feel quite relaxed about their shoes. And that's when I used to pounce; swiftly, deftly, expertly. A certain amount of crawling about on the floor was often required, but that went with the territory. I stole the shoes and I was gone. Later I'd imagine the women walking home shoeless, their bare feet exposed to the common gaze, and there was a certain sly pleasure in that too.

If I had taken you to my archive I would try to explain all this to you. Perhaps you would be looking at me a little askance by now – Catherine certainly was. But it would be time to press on. I would ask you to select a pair of shoes you liked and I would help you put them on. You would realize you were not the first to have worn them, that other women had been here as you were, and I would hope that the thought excited you.

We would enter the inner sanctum, the secret chamber, and I would draw the curtain closed behind us, so that we were in this enclosed space, the walls full of shoes, the ceiling mirrored, the floor lined with deep wool carpet. We would stand at the centre and I would undress us both. Perhaps you would have chosen a pair of red leather high-heeled mules with a peep-toe. I would kneel at your feet and kiss your flesh where it met the leather, then I would lay you down and fuck you long and intensely and tenderly, and no doubt you would look up, look past me, up at the mirrored ceiling, at our surroundings. And undoubtedly you would look at the rows of shoes, and you might think about all the past or future perverse acts these shoes represented. And with my cock inside you, with your feet encased in shoes of your own choosing, I would hope that you would finally be coming very close to understanding me. That, at least, is what I hoped for from Catherine, but perhaps I was asking too much, too soon.

Thirteen

You know those old movies where they're in a nightclub and the men are wearing evening dress and they have tiny spiv-like moustaches, and they're with some good-time girls, and then one of the guys pulls a shoe off one of the girl's feet and drinks champagne out of it? Well, come on, what's that all about? Is it meant to imply that the woman is so attractive that even the sweat from her feet is desirable? It could be a simple bit of self-degradation, but on the scale of human degradation it seems to be so low it's barely registering.

I'm far more persuaded that it's a symbolic act. The cad is drinking champagne from the woman's shoe, but really he wants to be drinking it from her cunt. Or maybe it's not really about drinking at all. You'll notice it's only ever champagne that gets drunk. Why isn't it a nice claret or a mature, tawny port? Well, I don't think there's much doubt it has something to do with ejaculation; white frothy stuff, not dark, resinous, full-bodied liquor. I suspect that it's pouring in the champagne that's the real symbolic act, not drinking it out.

The fact is, it's not all that easy to drink out of a woman's shoe, and I have of course tried. But for me the problem is more with the champagne than with the shoe. I'd much rather pour good, dark red wine over a woman's bare foot and then lick it off. That was something I frequently did with Catherine. It was another little foot-related eccentricity of mine, and she never complained. Besides, even good champagne can ruin a shoe, and we weren't going to take any risks, certainly not with Harold's handiwork.

Time passed. We kept visiting Harold and he kept coming up with the goods, producing pair after pair of wild and exquisite shoes. Catherine and I were delighted with everything he made, but it was never a simple or straightforward delight. There was always a dark edge to his work. One pair of black stiletto court shoes was studded with false eyes of the most intense powder blue. Another pair, made of vibrant red satin, had shards of smashed mirror set in the toe. Others featured strange and alarming fabrics: chain mail, semi-transparent rubber, antelope skin. Or there would be weird features and decoration; an ankle strap made out of sinister medical tubing, wooden heels carved into the shape of putti. Sometimes there would be asymmetrical rips and slashes in the fabric, designed to give tantalizing glimpses of the bare foot inside as Catherine walked.

We made a lot of visits to Harold's shop. Occasionally we'd arrive at the same time as one of his more orthodox customers, someone collecting a pair of handmade brogues or buckskin cricket boots. In that case we had to wait until he'd finished with them, then he'd shut the shop so that our business was entirely private. The world of fetishism had to be kept separate from his usual trade.

I sensed we were something special in Harold's life, but he seemed determined that we shouldn't become too friendly, and even though he lived in the flat above the shop, we were never invited there. Our transactions always took place in the neutral territory of the shop or workroom.

Owning truly great pairs of fetishistic shoes provokes at

least two important questions. One: where and on what occasions do you wear them? Two: what do you wear them with? The obvious answers might appear to be that you wear them every night in bed with nothing else at all, but Catherine and I wanted a less obvious answer.

Great feet and great shoes need to be shown off. A woman can wear killer FMs in her normal daily life, in the supermarket, at the pub, in the office. In these situations heads will definitely turn, the shoes may even be appreciated, but they only have that effect because they're actually out of place there. In fact, it was hard to think of anywhere, apart from a fetish club, where Harold's shoes *wouldn't* look out of place. So we decided to go to a fetish club.

It was called Stains, and its claim was that it 'celebrated sexual difference'. Of course, in one sense, a fetishist like myself actually wants to celebrate sexual similarity: the more closely feet and shoes resemble my own personal ideals the better I like them. But I knew what they meant. As far as I was aware, and naturally I'd done a little research on the subject, there was no club in London that catered just for foot and shoe fetishists, but we knew that dressing up in sexy gear, lethal high heels included, was one of the 'differences' that Stains celebrated, so it would have to do.

Harold's latest creation was a pair of peep-toed ankle boots made of what he assured us was monkeyskin. The ox-blood varnish on Catherine's toenails made a wicked contrast against the shaggy black fur of the shoe. Thus arose the problem of what else Catherine should wear. I wasn't surprised to learn that she'd been to one or two of these clubs before and she had a few well-chosen items in her wardrobe that would do the job; some wisps of leather and fishnet, a bit of exotic corsetry and uplift. It was powerful stuff, but for my tastes none of it was as wild or as eloquent as the shoes. As for me, I put on some leather trousers and a T-shirt with an illustration of a pair of FMs. It couldn't compete with Catherine's outfit, but it wasn't meant to.

These things are largely a matter of context. As we drove to the club in a taxi I felt that our get-up was ridiculously excessive, but the moment we entered the loud, low-ceilinged gloom of the club we seemed to stand out like a couple of arch conservatives. We were surrounded by wearers of ornate rubber, leather and PVC costumes that spoke only about sex. Bodies were encased and reshaped under the restraining influence of uniforms and wild fancy dress. The occasional set of bare breasts was visible, popping out of basques and through holes in rubber or leather bodysuits, and there were plenty of bare buttocks, both male and female. But little of the flesh on display was either natural or unmediated. Much of it was tattooed, and some of it was pierced. Rings and chains linked noses, nipples, ears and cheeks, and no doubt there were labia and penises that had come in for similar treatment, but they were covered – at least for the time being. All the props and paraphernalia of fetishistic sex were present and on display: whips and dildos, body harnesses, dog collars, mackintoshes; but the concentration and the diversity had a curiously diluting effect, as though one fetish cancelled out another.

Of course, one jumped to conclusions about the other people in the club. You read the costumes they had adorned themselves with and you made assumptions about whether they were gay or straight, submissive or dominant, voyeurs or exhibitionists. There was a smattering of male and female transvestism, and we saw someone in a nappy. This was undoubtedly the 'difference' we had been promised, but I wasn't sure how sexual, let alone erotic, it was. I made my Pavlovian responses to the various provocations around me, but men dressed as Shirley Bassey, gay boys in rubber shorts, women being led around on dog leads; these didn't hit the spot at all.

There was assertive, metallic music clanging through the place, but nobody was dancing. People preferred to strut and pose. Occasionally someone would stroke someone else's arm or cheek, or even bare bottom, yet the atmosphere was oddly without erotic charge, and it wasn't a pick-up joint as far as I could see. A few people came up and talked to us. They were friendly, and of course they were heavily dressed up, but there were no offers of sexual difference. We were simply asked whether this was the first time we'd been to Stains, and whether we were enjoying ourselves. It was simply an attempt to make new members feel welcome.

It seemed to me there were two distinct types of clientele. The first was young and glamorous, and for them this kind of dressing up was just another way of being fashionable. They were dressed more outrageously, and showed more of their exceptionally good bodies than they would have in a more ordinary nightclub, but it was still just a form of clubbing. It may have been sexy but it wasn't sex itself. The second type, generally the older ones, the middle-aged men with their pot bellies and leather masks, carrying their enema kits, and their women, with cellulite visible between their stocking-tops and leather panties, well, you knew they were serious about things. You knew they really meant it. The two groups had nothing in common and yet there was no antagonism between them. Even if old and young, attractive and ugly, bent and straight weren't exactly coming together, they were at least tolerating each other's existence. They were tolerating Catherine and me too, and I didn't think we fitted into either category.

101

Of course I checked out the shoes that the women around me were wearing, and you couldn't deny that people were making an effort. There was fiercely fetishistic footwear on all sides; the usual stuff, spike highs, viciously pointed toes, platforms, straps, laces, thongs, buckles. There were boots of all lengths, from ankle to upper, upper thigh. I enjoyed it but, if anything, the effect was too strident. Compared to the devastating eroticism of the shoes Catherine was wearing, all these others seemed a little crass and obvious. Not that crassness and obviousness was necessarily out of place at Stains; take the cabaret act that started halfway through the evening.

A man of about fifty with a scrawny but tanned body, that he was showing most of, was dragged on to a small stage by two women in dominatrix gear. They wheeled out a wooden apparatus, somewhat like stocks, somewhat like a rack, strapped the poor guy into it, and started to give him a mild but theatrical going over.

An audience gathered quickly around the stage and there was a lot of cheering and encouragement, but it was the sort of crowd that gawps at a freak show, not a crowd that comes together in celebration. The most spectacular 'torture' inflicted on the victim involved one of the women shoving the spiked heel of her shoe into the man's open mouth. This caused a lot of audience response, but it seemed to me to have more to do with sword swallowing than with shoe fetishism. It seemed to have nothing at all to do with sex.

The evening passed and it wasn't unenjoyable. Watching people is always entertaining, and much more so when they're so keen to be watched. And, of course, people scrutinized Catherine and me too. I'm sure nobody found me an object of any great fascination, but Catherine was much stared at and leched over. However, it was a general all-purpose kind of lechery. If someone had come up to her and offered to lick or suck her feet I would have been delighted and not surprised. But nobody did. At one point a slim, slightly camp young man with studded belts criss-crossing his chest came up and said he'd like, and I quote, 'To give both your arseholes a tongue bath,' and while this wasn't either the time or the place to be offended I did think he was missing the point. We declined.

Later I was invited into a dark area of the club where a dozen or so men were lining up to spank a blindfolded woman who was bent over a leather chair. Reluctantly, and only at Catherine's insistence, I went along and joined in, but my heart was never in it. I didn't enjoy spanking the woman and my performance was so perfunctory that I'm sure she didn't enjoy it very much either.

We left when another cabaret act started. Two women with shaven heads, in depressingly authentic-looking Nazi regalia, got up on stage and started licking each other's breasts. The breast licking I enjoyed, and the shaven heads were fine, but I found the Nazi regalia too hard to take.

I emerged from the club feeling strangely illiberal. It wasn't that I thought the membership of Stains should be prevented from enjoying, or persecuted because of, their unusual sexual preferences, but I thought they should just keep them to themselves.

When we got home Catherine and I made love, and even though Catherine kept the shoes on, and even though she ran them all over my face and body, it seemed an act of purest vanilla after what we'd seen in the club.

Then Catherine said, 'A strange thing happened on my way to the bathroom. A man came up to me, older man, not bad looking, normal looking, and he was carrying a

103

woman's shoe. He handed it to me, asked would I take it into the Ladies, piss into it, fill it up and then return it to him.'

'Are you serious?' I asked. I hadn't seen any man wandering around with a woman's shoe, and it was the kind of thing I'd have noticed.

'He was very serious,' said Catherine.

'What did you do?'

'What would you have wanted me to do?'

'I don't know,' I said. 'I really don't know.'

'Maybe you'll be disappointed in me. I told him he was disgusting. I said he should get a life.'

'What did he say?'

'He seemed to like being bad-mouthed. So I said I already had one pervert in my life and that was enough. And he said you were a very lucky man.'

'I know,' I said. 'I know I'm lucky.'

But luck can change.

Fourteen

I arrived at Catherine's flat in the usual way. I gave a firm, sustained ring on the front doorbell, a ring that meant business. She was expecting me and she let me in immediately. I knew she would be waiting, wearing a pair of Harold's shoes, ready for me as usual, ready to do the things that we always did. But this time there was going to be a difference. This time I wasn't alone. This time I had a female companion: Rosemary.

Rosemary and I went back a long way. Rosemary was no beauty, not even from the ankles down. She was heavily built, brassy, and she was in no conceivable sense my sort of woman. But she was supremely willing to try just about anything sexual, and there had been a number of times over the years when we, she and I, had had need of each other. This was just such an occasion. Today she was wearing a black raincoat and her rather plump feet were gamely crammed into a pair of purple velvet high heels. She had considered all other clothing unnecessary.

We stepped into the building, walked briskly up the stairs to Catherine's floor, then to her front door, which she had left open. We went inside, into the hall where Catherine was waiting. She did a double-take when she saw Rosemary, looked at her curiously, suspiciously, but she didn't speak. I imagine I was looking both furtive and pleased with myself, while Rosemary looked around the flat and its furnishings as though she might be a prospective purchaser or perhaps a burglar.

Catherine stared hard into Rosemary's round, painted face. For a moment she looked as though she was about to ask who this stranger was and what she was doing there, but explaining would have spoiled everything and, in any case, she was in no real doubt what was going on, or about to. I put a finger to her lips to hush her. I nodded to Rosemary and, as arranged, she shrugged the raincoat from her shoulders. She stood there naked apart from the purple velvet shoes; very white, unembarrassed, very lewd. Her breasts looked enormous, and Catherine and I could see that the colour of her pubic hair did not even remotely match that on her head.

The three of us went into the bedroom and there proceeded to do everything we wanted to and could possibly think of. I suppose a certain amount of it might be considered predictable. The combination of mouths, organs, fluids, feet and shoes are, inevitably, limited. However much one strives to be inventive there are only so many options, so many possibilities. Nevertheless we achieved a number of combinations and conjunctions that I, at least, had never managed before.

It was a long session, hot and exhausting. When it was all over, when Rosemary had put her raincoat on again and gone, she left her shoes behind as a sort of souvenir, and suffice it to say that they were thoroughly sodden with both male and female juices.

Catherine and I lay together feeling emptied, carved out. It seemed to me there was nothing to be said about what we'd done, no room and no reason for discussion. But Catherine said, 'I think that may have been too much.'

'What?' I asked.

'I think that may have been a "this far and no further."'

Catherine turned away from me slightly, gathered herself to herself.

'That was the most obscene stuff I've ever done,' she continued. 'It was more obscene than anything I would ever have imagined myself capable of doing.'

I had not been consciously testing Catherine. I had not been pushing at limits, extending boundaries, seeing how far we could go, how far I could take her with me. Yet I was sensible enough to realize that bringing Rosemary along to participate in our sex life was some new high-water mark. I could understand that someone might think this episode had been conceived of as an act of transgression, of desecration, a conscious smashing of the rules, but I hadn't imagined that Catherine would be that someone.

'Is that such a bad thing?' I asked.

'I think it may be,' she said.

'I don't see what the problem is,' I said. 'You certainly looked like you were enjoying yourself.'

'Of *course* I looked like I was enjoying myself. I *was* enjoying myself. That's what the problem is. That's why I think it may have been too much. I think I may have gone too far.'

At the time I thought she was exaggerating, and I didn't believe her; but I should have.

Fifteen

There is one woman whose feet I really would like to see, or to have seen. Her name is Marjorie Howard and her feet are something of a legend. In the 1920s, D.W. Griffith, who was apparently something of a foot man himself, got together with the legendary shoemaker Salvatore Ferragamo and ran a competition to find the most beautiful feet in Hollywood. The first prize was to be a six-month film contract and runners-up got shoes made by Ferragamo. Marjorie Howard is the woman who won the contest. Both she and her feet are now lost to history, but second prize went to the then unknown Joan Crawford. She was trying desperately to break into the movies, and entering a beauty contest for feet must have seemed as good a way as any other.

Now, I've seen photographs of Joan Crawford's feet, or, at least, photographs of Joan Crawford in which her feet appear, and I'd have to say they were not really prize-winning feet. There are no obvious deformities, the toes are nice and straight, they appear well looked after, but they're a little fleshy for my tastes, and the big toes are a little on the bulbous side. OK, so I know that beauty contests are an insult to womanhood and, at the very least, highly subjective, and perhaps I wouldn't have adored Marjorie Howard's feet, but I'd like to have had the chance.

As a matter of fact, if you read Ferragamo's autobiography, *Shoemaker of Dreams*, he says he preferred Joan Crawford's feet, anyway, but I'm not sure Ferragamo is a man you can always trust. He says the Duchess of Windsor and Susan Hayward both had perfect feet. He says Alicia Markova's feet were 'strong and lovely and startling.' He says Mary Pickford's feet were 'lovely'. Greta Garbo's feet were just 'beautiful', while Marlene Dietrich, he says, was the possessor of 'the most beautiful feet in the world.'

I guess that if you were a great shoemaker then you'd tend to attract women with wonderful feet, but I suspect that Ferragamo was a bit of a flatterer. If you were rich enough to be able to afford a pair of his shoes, then he'd be happy to say you had beautiful feet too. He made shoes for Clara Petacci and Eva Braun but he doesn't tell us much about what their feet were like.

And he also made shoes for Pola Negri. I have read (in her obituary actually) that she was the first actress ever to paint her toenails. This seems unlikely to me. Surely civilization didn't need so many millennia to invent such an apparently obvious cosmetic effect. But I'm in no position to argue, and I've never seen a close-up of Pola Negri's bare feet any more than I've seen those of Marjorie Howard, but I'd like to think that a woman who invented toenail painting must have had good feet, or at least good toenails.

The world of movies and movie stars is a strange one where feet are concerned. Movie stars are almost always beautiful. Their faces and bodies are whipped into shape by experts: makeup artists, personal trainers, plastic surgeons; and, although I'm sure their feet aren't entirely neglected, they're not the things by which stars are rated and judged, except by me.

Actresses are photographed the whole time. You can buy whole books of photographs of Marilyn Monroe or

Charlotte Rampling or Rita Hayworth or Madonna. When we look at these photographs, even if we look with whole-hearted admiration and approval, we are still subjecting these women to intense critical scrutiny. I just happen to scrutinize the feet rather than anything else.

Having browsed through a number of books on Marilyn Monroe I've found that her feet have left me curiously unmoved. In lots of ways this is a pity. Her wiggle may or may not have been caused by the high heels she wore (some say it was because of an ankle deformity), and she did allegedly once say, 'It was the high heel that gave a big lift to my career.' Her feet are nice enough, but they're curiously wholesome and unsexy, and her choice of shoes, or at least the shoes she was forced to wear in films, was poor. For example, in that scene from *The Seven Year Itch* where her skirt blows up, the legs are great and the skirt is great, the cleavage and the face are great, but she's wearing some dreary white open sandals that do nothing for her or for me.

Helen Mirren is an actress who shot up in my estimation when, a long time ago now, I read an article in which she confessed to having a thing about shoes. The article, need-less to say, is given pride of place in the archive, and I can quote it from memory. 'I can't seem to throw them away,' she says. 'No matter how battered and worn they might be. I go into a shop to buy something sensible to wear to rehearsals and come out clutching a pair of stilettos.' Then she talks about her latest acquisition, a pair of black court shoes from Seditionaries with studs embedded in the heels, and says, 'They really worry people, you know. I think that is a mark of an exceptional pair of shoes.' How true that is. The article is illustrated with Helen lying on her stomach on a glass table surrounded by shoes. Lord have mercy.

Here is Britt Ekland in her book *Sensual Beauty and How to Achieve It*:

> I believe a good-looking foot is as important as a good-looking hand. I'm not saying there is necessarily anything very sensual about feet, [Shame on you, Britt!] but after all they have been known to touch a man's lips, and obviously in the dark the poor soul isn't going to know what he's reaching for, so it's really up to you. If that's the kind of intimate relationship you have, you have to keep your feet lovable.

I'm not sure whether it's Britt's dodgy grasp of English or her lack of a good ghost writer that makes this paragraph so impenetrable, but you sort of know what she means, and at least she seems to have some inkling of what foot sex is about. Britt, I would say, on the evidence of the photographs in *Sensual Beauty*, has feet you definitely wouldn't kick out of bed. In some of the photographs they look a touch wrinkled, the little toenail is slightly gnarled and shapeless, but hey, the photographs are blown up pretty large. How many feet could bear that close an inspection? Well, Catherine's could, of course, but not so many others.

Again, although Britt is usually happy to get her kit off, I'm pretty sure that her feet have never actually figured large in a movie. I'm not absolutely sure because I haven't seen her entire *oeuvre*, and frankly I don't want to. I'm not a complete idiot. I wouldn't go to see a movie simply in the hope of seeing Britt Ekland's feet, or anyone else's, and I'm perfectly happy to see a film that has no feet in it at all. But if I'm sitting there in the dark watching a movie and suddenly there is some element of pedic sexuality, if an actress walks across the frame in high heels, or is given a foot massage by her lover or goes into a shoe shop or gets a pedicure, then it does tend to swamp my response to the rest of the film.

Here is J. G. Ballard on the subject:

> With the resources of video, you can build up quite a large library of images . . . I can imagine that, quite accidentally, you might get some obsessive, say, who finds himself collecting footage of women's shoes whenever they're shown (it doesn't matter if it's Esther Williams walking around a swimming pool with forties sound, or Princess Di) – he presses his button and records all this footage of women's shoes . . . After accumulating two hundred hours of shoes, you might have a bizarre obsessive movie that's absolutely riveting.

You might. You might indeed. And I have tried, God knows I've tried, but it's surprisingly hard. All too often the image has been and gone before you've reached for the remote control and pressed the record button. I am no techno freak, nevertheless my archive contained a certain amount of video material, and I sometimes edited together relevant images and, if I say so myself, some of the results weren't bad.

It was always a work in progress, but here's one way it might have run. Fade in on Mickey Rourke sprawled on a bed stroking Kim Basinger's feet in *9½ Weeks*, then cut to Dirk Bogarde doing the same with Charlotte Rampling in *The Night Porter*, but here they're on the floor and he's actually kissing them, then to *Bull Durham* where Kevin Costner is painting Susan Sarandon's toenails, cut to Goldie Hawn in *Overboard* where her manservant is doing the same for her. Then the shot from *Who's That Girl*, where Madonna's just been transformed from the street urchin to the glamour puss and we see her for the first time in a spangly ball gown, and the camera starts at her feet then moves all the way up her body to her face, but in my version we do a freeze frame on the start of the shot, the first moment when Madonna's feet fill the whole screen. Madonna, incidentally, has feet to die for. Cut to Ava Gardner in *The Barefoot Contessa*, cut to the scene in *The War of the Roses* where Danny De Vito's girlfriend starts to give him a foot job under the dinner table. Possibly then a collage of images from *Single White Female* where first we see the girls trying on and buying metal-heeled, black suede court shoes, several shots of these shoes pacing corridors, then finally (and not too credibly in my opinion) the scene where Jennifer Jason Leigh kills Bridget Fonda's boyfriend by driving one of the heels into his eye. Changing the pace, we have a brief shot of Katherine Helmond in *Brazil* wearing a leopardskin shoe on her head, an idea borrowed from Elsa Schiaparelli, then Alan Howard stroking Helen Mirren's feet in *The Cook, The Thief, His Wife and Her Lover*.

I could go on and on, but for now I'd end with the shot from Buñuel's *L'Age d'Or*, when Lya Lys, in a state of sexual arousal and frustration, sucks the toe of a statue of Christ. Her lips are a perfect shiny black against the white stone of the statue, and her eyes look glazed and orgasmic. It is one of the most truly pornographic images I know. The only problem with this, of course, is that it's a man's toe she's sucking and that is well outside my range of interests.

Quite early on with Catherine, after I'd been sucking her feet for a while, she decided to return the favour and took my big toe in her mouth and moved her lips back and forth over it in a perfect impersonation of fellatio. It was a thoughtful gesture, I suppose, but I was appalled. I had to tell her to stop. My feet and toes are probably better looking than a good many men's but I couldn't possibly let a woman

113

suck them. It was a disgusting idea. As I said to Catherine, 'I may be a fetishist but I'm not a sicko.' At the time she believed me, but later she seemed to change her mind.

Sixteen

A moment came when I knew something was wrong.
Catherine phoned me – a rare event in itself – and she
wanted to meet. This wasn't exactly breaking the rules, but
it wasn't the way we normally did things. I was the one who
usually made the running. And then she said she wanted to
meet on neutral territory. She suggested London Zoo.

'As neutral as that,' I said, and I feared the worst.

It was a cool grey day and the zoo wasn't crowded. We
met by the aquatic birds of Europe and I saw at once it was
worse than I could have expected. Catherine was wearing
a pair of trainers. They were possibly very expensive and
fashionable and loaded with statements about status and
fitness and youth, but I was hearing a very different statement. She wanted to walk and talk.

'I think it's over,' she said. 'I think something's happened.'

I suppose it didn't come as a complete surprise but that
didn't make it hurt any the less.

'What sort of thing?' I asked as coolly as I could.

'I don't know exactly, but I know I can't carry on like
this.'

'Like what?'

'You know what I'm talking about.'

Maybe I did and maybe I didn't. Either way I wanted to
hear her name it, to spell it out, but at first she wouldn't
or couldn't.

'You know,' she said. 'I just ask myself, and I think you should ask yourself too, is this a sensible way for two adults to conduct their lives?'

'For me it's the only way,' I said.

'I'm not even sure if I believe that. But for me it's *not* the only way.'

'Lucky old you,' I said. 'Was it bringing Rosemary to your flat that did it?'

'It didn't help.'

'OK,' I said. 'It was just a one off. It was a variation. We tried it and you didn't like it, so, fine, we won't do it again.'

'It wasn't only that.'

'Was it showing you the archive?'

'The archive is pretty strange, you have to admit.'

'OK, I'll admit it if that helps. Was it Harold and his shoes?'

'Harold's pretty strange too.'

'Creepy you said.'

'Yes, he's creepy, but he does make nice shoes.'

'He does.'

We had arrived at the primates. The monkeys were throwing themselves at the wire fronts of their cages, playing to the gallery, showing off, mouths flapping with what you know is not laughter. Caged animals, the stuff of metaphor, the stuff of overworked imagery. Nature bound and perverted. I thought of the monkeyskin shoes Harold had made for Catherine. It was as if the whole zoo was a source of raw materials for shoemaking.

'So it's all got too strange and creepy for you, has it?' I said.

'Something like that.'

'I've scared you?'

'Something has.'

'You know,' I said sadly and calmly, 'I'll never find any-one who has feet as perfect as yours.'

'That may or may not be true,' she said. 'But either way, so what? I mean, be real, what does it matter whether or not a woman has beautiful feet? What does it *mean*?'

That could have got me very angry, but everything seemed to depend on staying cool, on remaining in control, of myself if not of the situation.

'It doesn't *mean* anything at all,' I said reasonably. 'That's the whole point. Beauty never does mean anything. Beauty is just a fact. It has no moral dimension. It has no conse-quence in itself. But in this case it has some consequences for me. I see a beautiful pair of feet and I want to act in a certain way. And that's all that matters. The fact that it matters to me.'

She turned away.

'Don't turn away,' I said. 'Would it do any good to say I love you?'

'But you don't,' she snapped. 'I don't even know if you like me. You're obsessed with my feet, but then, you're obsessed with everybody's feet.'

'Not true!' I protested, but she took no notice.

'I'm not stupid,' she continued. 'I'm not demanding the full-blown romantic love thing, but in general I don't think you can love a person just for their feet, much less for their shoes.'

'Can't you?'

'No, I don't think you can. Really. Look, I know this is no time to start quoting Spinoza . . .'

'You're going to quote Spinoza?'

'Sort of. I did a course in college. It's no big deal. It's just that he says love is a desire for unification with the other.

117

And I'll buy that. It sounds like sense to me. You can be unified with a person. You can't be unified with a foot or a shoe, can you?'

'Can't you?'

She spread her hands in a gesture of denial, to say that if I didn't understand something as simple as that, then I was even more stupid than she thought.

'So you're leaving because of Spinoza.'

'I'm leaving because of me.'

'OK, so let's talk about you.'

A regretful turn of the head, a stiffening of the body, a facial expression that said she knew all along it would have to come to this.

'I have a problem,' she said. 'I think there are several problems I might have. But I'm so confused by all this stuff that I don't know which of them is the real one.'

'So talk me through the possibilities.'

'OK. I've made a few notes.'

I couldn't believe it. She took a tiny, ringbound notepad from her pocket and opened it. I could see a lot of dense black writing slashed with arrows and crossings out, starred with asterisks, edged with doodles. She didn't exactly read from it but she referred to it often.

'OK,' she said. 'One: I have often thought of myself as a sexual adventurer, adventuress, whatever. And at first you were an adventure. A foot and shoe fetishist was a novelty. But fetishism isn't an adventure in itself. In itself it's just strange and obsessional and repetitive. Sometimes I think maybe I'm just bored with this particular adventure and it's time to move on.'

She said it in a detached way, as if reciting a case history or exploring a bit of character motivation in a film review.

'But you only think that sometimes,' I said.

'Yes,' she agreed. 'Sometimes I think, two: maybe I'm not as much of an adventuress as I thought I was. Maybe you've taken me too far, too fast. Maybe I only want to *play* at being an adventuress, only want to have little adventures. This stuff with the archive, this stuff with Rosemary, with Harold, with shoes in department stores, with pedicurists, with coming in my shoes, maybe you're too serious, too extreme an adventure for me.'

'It doesn't feel that way to me,' I said. 'I think you're a real adventuress all right.'

'Yes?' she said. 'In that case we can come to option three: maybe what's happened is that you've shown me that I'm even more of an adventuress than I thought I was. I've done things with you that I've never done with anybody else. It's been scary but it's also been pleasurable. And the scariest part is just *how* pleasurable. Maybe I've recognized that I could go all the way, whatever that means, could go a long way too far, and maybe I'm drawing back because I'm just sane enough to see how crazy I could be. If I carried on with you I don't know where it would end.'

I nodded, but I was agreeing with the theoretical position, not agreeing that this was necessarily the case with Catherine and me.

'Or maybe there's another answer,' she said. 'Maybe I'm not really any sort of sexual adventuress at all. Maybe I really *do* want the full-blown romantic love thing. And I realize this is going to sound dumb to you, but maybe I do want to be loved for myself.'

I was tempted to go all philosophical and sixth form on her and ask how she defined 'self', but I thought better of it.

Catherine said, 'But again, either way, whichever way, it makes no difference. Either way, I'm calling it off. Don't

119

phone me. Don't try to see me. If you really want to hate me, just think of me as a stupid, scared woman who simply got cold feet.'

Seventeen

At first I was very good. I was decent and I behaved myself. I respected Catherine, her needs and her feelings, and I did exactly as she asked. I stayed away, didn't bother her, didn't phone, however much I wanted to. And phoning was the least of what I wanted to do. I wanted to beg and scream, throw tantrums, camp on her doorstep until she saw the error of her ways. But I knew that none of that would do me any good; it would only confirm to her that she'd made no error at all. So I behaved myself.

Catherine's detailed consideration of her possible reasons for ending our relationship didn't make much impression on me. All or any of it might or might not have been true, but what difference did it make? However you looked at it there was something about me, or about me together with her, that she didn't like and didn't want. Not being able to put her finger precisely on the reason was neither here nor there. She simply didn't like things as they were. That was hard on me because I was perfectly happy, ecstatically happy, with things as they were, as they had been. The archive, the department store, Harold, Rosemary, it was all just fine with me. There was no point saying, let's work it out, let's try to make things different, since I absolutely didn't want things to be any different.

As for whether, as I had so rashly stated, I loved Catherine, well, I thought by any number of criteria I probably did. Maybe I didn't want to be unified with her *à la* Spinoza, but I certainly wanted to be with her. I wanted to be with her because she had perfect feet, and when I was with her I could partake of them. And you might say I *only* loved her for her feet but, as previously discussed, you have to love somebody for one reason or another, and in my book having perfect feet is a better reason than most. And if I did love her, it wasn't simply because she *possessed* the feet, it was because of what she did with them, what she let me do with them, how she presented them.

But something had changed in the presentation, and it wasn't only the trainers. A couple of days after our outing to the zoo the postman brought a package containing all the pairs of shoes Harold had made for Catherine. She had sent them back. I had bewilderingly mixed feelings about that. Of course I wanted to have the shoes. They were glorious and exquisite works of art, and few people in the world were better equipped to appreciate them than I was. They would become a treasured part of the archive. But, as I had always said, as Harold had agreed, shoes without feet in them are only half alive, and these particular shoes, in the absence of their perfect wearer, were intensely melancholy reminders of what had been and gone. There was no way I would ever be able to ask some other woman to wear them, so they were destined never to have a full life at all. Their presence in the archive would cause me some pain, but the idea of Catherine keeping the shoes and wearing them as she participated in some new adventures with somebody else would have been far worse. I wanted them safe with me.

Nevertheless, I didn't think I could just put them straight into the archive. I thought I had a duty to offer to give them back to Harold. Even though they had been his freely given gift, I still felt that he had some rights over them. So I went along to his shop at the end of a working day, feeling obligated to make the offer, but passionately hoping it was an offer he'd refuse. And, of course, I had to explain the reason I was making the offer, that Catherine had ended our relationship. I did my confused best to make him understand something that I barely understood myself. His reaction was extreme and unexpected. His face sagged as though it was caving in on itself. He started to bawl like a child and beat his fists against his workbench.

'Hey, Harold, it's not that bad,' I said, thinking it was absurd that I had to comfort him for what was supposed to be my own grief. 'These things happen.'

'They happen to me all the time,' Harold said. 'First Ruth gets taken away from me, and now Catherine. It's just not fair. It's not right. If I don't have anyone to make shoes for, I'm not sure I have any reason to live.'

I didn't like the renewed talk of suicide, and neither did I like the way he seemed to be thinking of his Ruth and my Catherine as equivalents. I said, 'Come on, Harold. I think you're overreacting a little here.'

But he didn't think so at all. He was inconsolable, and my desire to console him was only partial. If anything, I had imagined that he might try to console *me*. I let him bawl a little longer. It was a while before he was able to pull himself together, and when he did he asked, 'Did she leave you for another man?'

'No,' I said.

'That's a pity,' said Harold. 'Sometimes being left for someone else can make it easier. At least that way you can channel all your anger and hatred in one specific direction.'

Harold appeared to be speaking with an authority I didn't imagine him to have. He didn't look like much of a player in the world of feeling, and I certainly didn't agree with him. My anger didn't need any channelling, didn't need any focus, and if Catherine had left me for someone else I was sure I'd have felt a hundred times worse.

'No, she didn't leave me for anyone else,' I confirmed.

'At least, that's what she told you.'

I wasn't going to go down that path, so I asked him what I'd come to ask: did he want me to give back the shoes he'd made for Catherine. To my relief he didn't. He said it was the process that was important to him, not the finished product. I couldn't agree with that either, although it didn't matter now whether or not Harold and I saw eye to eye.

I noticed there was a work in progress on his bench, a shoe Catherine would never wear, a design he would never finish. The raw materials consisted of a length of what looked like fox fur, a strip of razor wire and some high heels carved out of bone. I could just about imagine what kind of shoes Harold would have made out of these materials, and yet I knew that if he had completed the work it would have exceeded all my expectations.

I left Harold as I had seen him once or twice before, slumped at his workbench, head in hands, distress and misery oozing from him. Even though I resented his usurpation of what I thought was my own personal loss, I still felt that I had taken much more from him than I could ever possibly give back, something much bigger and more personal than the shoes he'd made. I left him, left the shop. I couldn't think when or in what circumstances I would ever see him again.

Eighteen

I went to Mike and Natasha's house. They didn't know that I'd split up with Catherine because I hadn't told them. And even if they had known, they wouldn't have seen it as a very significant event. They would have regarded it as an all too regular and ordinary occurrence in my life. The three of us were supposed to be going out for a cheap Italian meal, but Mike opened the door and said there'd been a change of plan.

'Natasha's not feeling so good,' he said.

'Nothing serious?'

'No, no, but she says we should go without her.'

He was wearing his jacket and was all ready to set off. I never even stepped inside the house, never saw Natasha. We went without her but we didn't get as far as the Italian restaurant. Mike wanted to stop for a beer on the way, at some dingy crowded pub that I'd never been to before, and it was obvious that he had some serious drinking to do. The occasional need for oblivion was one that I'd always understood, the more so since Catherine's departure, though I didn't know what had stirred the need in Mike. It was a long time before he got round to telling me. We'd had several pints, and had abandoned all hope of getting anything to eat, before Mike admitted there was anything wrong at all.

Finally he said, 'It's me and Natasha. Or rather, it's just me.'

Mike and Natasha seemed perfectly happy together but it didn't surprise me there might be problems; after all they were human, weren't they?

'It's a big one,' Mike continued. 'A big, serious, potentially terminal kind of thing.'

'Really?' I said. I thought he must be exaggerating. Whatever the problem, I couldn't imagine the two of them splitting up, and I couldn't imagine the problem was anything like as important or as intractable as that which had driven Catherine and me apart.

Mike said, 'You know the way I sometimes say let's buy some drugs and pick up a couple of harlots?'

'It's one of your more endearing traits,' I said.

'Well, I did it.'

'You did?'

'Well, there was no cocaine involved and it was only one harlot.'

I expect I looked at him in some disbelief, but he obviously wasn't making it up.

'It was in Birmingham,' he explained. 'I was there on business. I was sitting at the hotel bar and so was she. We got talking and I bought her a drink and one thing led to another.'

I nodded. It seemed commonplace enough, though obviously it was a complete novelty in Mike's life; in mine too for that matter.

'Does Natasha know?' I asked.

'I haven't told her but she knows something's wrong. Do you think I should tell her?'

'No,' I said. 'What good would it do?'

'Confession. Good for the soul.'

'Very bad for a marriage,' I said.

'How would you know? How would you know anything about marriage?'

He was right. I had no more right to comment on marriage than I thought Harold had to comment on love and loss.

'I'm just taking an educated guess,' I said.

He gave the matter some thought, then nodded to himself as though he'd decided I might know what I was talking about after all.

'She wouldn't understand,' he said.

'I think she'd understand perfectly, but that's not necessarily a good thing,' I said. 'Besides, what's to understand? You got drunk and did something you regret.'

He shook his head. 'No, you don't understand. I don't regret it at all,' he said. 'It was the best fun I've ever had in my whole life. It was great. We did all sorts of things I'd never done before, really dirty stuff that Natasha would never do.'

'Do I really need this much detail?' I asked.

'There was no love, no affection, no respect for the other person. It was dirty and cheap and disgusting and degrading. And I loved it. I absolutely loved it.'

'Oh shit,' I said.

'And I want to do it again. I want to do it right now, and keep on doing it, every night of the week for the rest of my life.'

'And where does Natasha fit in?'

'That's what I don't know.'

'You're still in love with her?'

'Of course I'm still in love with her. I care for her. I cherish her. I respect her. And that's why our sex life is so fucking dull.'

'Oh shit,' I said.

'Oh shit, indeed.'

We sat quietly amidst the noise and smoke of the pub, in a little pod of gloom. Confession had not been good for Mike, it had made him profoundly miserable. But he pulled himself together enough to get up, go to the bar and order a couple more numbing drinks. I was feeling miserable too, and no longer just because of Catherine. I felt sorry for Mike, even more so for Natasha. It wasn't simply that I wanted them to be happy and together, it was more that Mike's confession had been so depressingly, destructively sordid.

'It's OK,' Mike said when he returned. 'I'm not asking you to solve anything for me.'

'Just as well.'

Mike took a big drink from his glass, then said, 'Right, now it's your turn.'

'What do you mean?'

'I've shown you mine, now you show me yours.'

'I'm not with you.'

'You know what I mean. You've got some dark little secret, haven't you? Natasha and I have always wondered about it. What is it you're into? Pain? Little girls? Little boys?'

'You don't really think I'm into children?'

'I don't know what you're into. So tell me.'

So I told him. I don't know exactly why I did. I had no particular desire to be understood by Mike, and I didn't feel that his confession had put any obligation on me. It had far more to do with what was going on in my own life. Maybe I was compensating. Maybe what I really wanted to do was pour my heart out over Catherine, and talking about my fetishism was just an easy way of avoiding the issue. Whatever the reason, I told him. Not in the kind of detail, nor with the kind of relish that I'd told Catherine on our first meeting, but I recounted my story as honestly as I knew how. I explained what I liked and what I did, though I said nothing at all about Catherine. Mike listened in a distracted way, staring into his beer, twisting the glass around in both hands. A look of puzzlement and mild amusement flickered across his face from time to time, and when I'd said all I was going to, he looked at me and said, 'Bullshit.'

'What?'

'You don't have to mess around with me,' he said.

'I'm not messing around.'

'It's a wind-up, isn't it? You don't really expect me to believe all that. You don't expect me to take that crap seriously.'

'Well, yes, I guess I do,' I said feeling insulted and not at all defensive.

I think it wasn't until then that he believed me at all. He really had found it inconceivable that anyone, least of all one of his friends, could feel the way I did about feet and shoes. It was a new idea, an undreamed of possibility. When he'd finally, reluctantly, taken it on board he said, 'Well, that's just pathetic.'

He started to laugh. It was sniggering, contemptuous, destructive laughter. I thought he was in danger of standing up and making an announcement to the whole pub about precisely how pathetic he thought I was.

'You really are a pitiful specimen, aren't you?' he said.

'Hey, Mike, you don't have to like it.'

'No, I bloody don't.'

I couldn't understand why he was so angry and affronted. What would he have done if I really *had* been into pain or little girls? Probably he could have accepted that more easily. Perhaps he'd expected something more dramatic, more 'dirty' and more in keeping with his own newly developed tastes. Perhaps he'd hoped that I was a kindred spirit. He gave me a look of definitive contempt and got up from his seat.

'I'm going to find myself a good old-fashioned whore,' he said. 'That's something you'd know nothing about.'

It was perfectly true at the time.

Nineteen

I tried to carry on as normal. I went to work, I went out sometimes, though it appeared I wasn't going to be seeing much of Mike and Natasha from now on. That made me sad too, but I tried to get on with my life, and it certainly wasn't easy. It even crossed my mind that I should take to the streets again with my clipboard and camera and try to find new pairs of feet and shoes that would excite me. But I didn't. It would have felt sacrilegious. And again, even though my archive was now all the richer for the addition of Catherine's shoes (or Harold's shoes, I wasn't quite sure of the correct terminology), I didn't spend a lot of time with it. My thoughts were elsewhere. Let's face it, my thoughts were all over the place.

There were times when I tried to imagine where Catherine was and what she was doing, but it was impossible. Her life was and always had been a mystery to me. I had no idea what she did or who she saw when she wasn't with me. She described herself as an adventuress and it wouldn't have surprised me to learn that she was off having adventures. Unlike Harold, I didn't want to have this stuff made specific and personal. I didn't want to know. And why should I have to? London was surely big enough for me not to run across Catherine by chance. I wasn't sure precisely how I would react if I did happen to see her, but I suspected I wouldn't emerge with much dignity. And I was right.

It was night and I was in my car. I'd stopped at traffic lights and a red car, something Japanese and low to the ground, pulled up behind me. I looked in my rear-view mirror and immediately saw that Catherine was the passenger in the car. I couldn't believe it. I felt as though someone had poured a bucket of hot fat over me. Then I looked at the driver. He was a young, dark, smooth-skinned man with a lot of black curly hair. I stared into the mirror with growing panic as Catherine leaned over and kissed him.

That's when I lost it. Some circuit burned out, some trip switch was thrown inside me. The traffic lights changed, and, without quite understanding what I was doing or why, I slowed down so that the red car was forced to overtake me. As it accelerated past I saw Catherine more clearly. She looked happy, alive, drunk, and she was far too engrossed in her new man to notice me or recognize my car. So I started to follow them. I suppose I wanted to see where they were going, to know what new life Catherine had pitched herself into, though I had no idea what I'd do once I had that knowledge.

The man drove erratically, sometimes too fast, sometimes dawdling. I guessed he was drunk too. At last he turned off the main road, went into a side street, stopped abruptly and parked his car a long way from the kerb. The engine and lights were switched off and the two of them got out. I drove slowly past and stopped a safe distance away.

The street was dark and empty. It was lined with big, old, grey buildings that had once been dignified and substantial, but now some were empty and others had been converted into less dignified enterprises; a wine warehouse, a printer's, a plumber's supply shop. It didn't look like a place where anyone would live, but the man felt in his pocket for a key and made for a door next to the printer's.

Catherine took his arm, and kissed him with real, if deliberately exaggerated, passion. He responded and then pulled away laughing. He opened the door, they went in. I saw a series of lights go on up the flights of stairs, all the way to the top floor, which I supposed was a converted flat above the shop.

Once I was sure they were safely inside, I went over to the door and read the name on the doorbell. It was Kramer, an innocent enough name, I thought at the time. I waited all night in my car, and I didn't sleep. I had the radio on, jammed between stations, picking up Cuban rhythms, Creole languages, flurries of static and Morse code. I kept my eyes trained on the windows of the flat. A light was on but there were no shadows on the curtain, no hint of movement, nothing to tell me what was going on in there. All that was left to my imagination. I had to invent new obscenities and pornographies for the two of them to commit on each other, and my powers of invention had never been greater.

It was a long, long night. When dawn seeped in between the buildings I was still expecting nothing. I thought a time would eventually come when someone would draw back the curtains of Kramer's flat, and I would see a face, it could be his or hers, looking blurred and sated. But I imagined that still to be some hours away. Then, against all expectations, the front door started to open. I didn't dare to hope it was Catherine, and yet even before she appeared I knew it had to be her. She was alone and she was badly ruffled. Her face, her hair, her whole body looked creased and worn. Her dress was too thin for the cold of the morning. She hugged her arms around herself and started to walk down the street, heading in my direction, slowly, cautiously, as though the ground was not to be trusted.

Her legs were bare, paler and leaner than I remembered. The knees looked rough and were reddened, as though she had been kneeling in front of him, or been dragged across a carpet, or been crawling on all fours. Then I looked at her feet. They were bare except for the coat of enamel on her toenails, and I watched them flatten themselves against the cold roughness of the pavement, watched them arch and spring as they took her along the dirty, unswept street.

She looked hungover, or perhaps still drunk. She seemed raw, exposed, sand-papered, and yet she was wholly self-contained. Nothing was going to get to her. It must have been then that she realized I was watching her. She must have known. She might have recognized the car, might even have seen me behind the wheel, my face blurred and streaked behind the windscreen. She didn't appear to react, but what she did next, she must certainly have done for my benefit.

She continued to walk down the street towards me, gathering momentum and confidence. She walked purposefully until she was ten or twelve feet from my car and then she stopped dead. There was a big, soft, fresh curl of dog shit lying directly in her path. She teetered a little, and I assumed she had stopped to avoid it, but then she looked hard in my direction, made a movement of her body that had some hint of a curtsy about it, and then she placed her bare right foot down firmly into the dog shit.

It submitted to the pressure. It spread, extended its boundaries, curled around the sides of her feet, oozed up between her toes like swamp mud or chocolate spread. And she took her right foot out of the shit and did exactly the same thing with her left. She was smiling to herself, feeling the warm slime of the shit on her soles, enjoying the sweet filthiness of the experience.

She stopped looking in my direction and began to move on, staring down at her feet as she walked, turning back to look at the shitty brown footprints she was leaving behind her. She seemed pleased with the effect and walked straight past me without looking back.

My face felt as though it was being pressed into hot coals. There were pains in my chest, and my hands were trembling. I wanted to kill something, tear something apart with my bare hands, with my teeth. I wanted to consume blood, rotting meat, raw jellyfish. I wanted to swallow lumps of the world and vomit them up again. But there was a much simpler remedy. I slipped my cock out of my trousers and needed only a few savage pulls on my foreskin before I shot sperm all over the dashboard.

Twenty

I went home. The next few days were hell. I hated myself. I had no belief in the healing powers of time. I knew that I could not and did not want to forget Catherine. Yet although I didn't want to get rid of her memory, I *did* want to quell the pain of remembering. So I found myself doing a number of things that I would previously have considered out of character. Visiting a prostitute was the first of these.

No doubt I wouldn't have done it if Mike's Birmingham exploits hadn't been on my mind. I thought maybe I could be like him, detached from the person he loved, relishing emptiness and dirt. I found her card in a phone box. The card was sunshine yellow, there was a drawing of high heels on it, and the unpunctuated selling line, 'Love me love my feet.'

I called the number and spoke to a woman with a smoker's cough and a Geordie accent.

'I'm calling about the ad,' I said.

'And which ad would that be?'

'Love me love my feet,' I said.

'Would you like to make an appointment to meet the young lady?'

'I think so. Probably yes.'

'The young lady is called Alicia. She's a lovely girl, dark haired, large chest, could easily be mistaken for a model.'

'How about her feet?'

'Lovely feet, sir. Lovely.'

I wasn't going to let her get away with anything so glib. Eroticism is about specifics.

'I need more detail,' I said and the woman started giving me some ball-park figures regarding Alicia's hourly rates. These sounded both vague and extortionate, but I said, 'That all sounds fine, really fine, but what I need is for you to describe her feet.'

'Are you taking the piss?' the voice rasped.

'No,' I said. 'Definitely not. I saw the ad and I do love feet, but I'm particular. Not any foot will do. If I get there and find Alicia has the wrong kind of feet, then I'll have wasted everybody's time.'

'We don't like time-wasters, sir.'

'Of course not.'

'Once you were here we would insist on your paying the fee whether you liked the young lady or not.'

'That's why I need you to describe the feet now. Please.'

Somewhat grudgingly she said, 'The young lady has wonderful white, smooth, creamy feet. Very lovely, very kissable.'

I still wasn't very convinced. It sounded to me as though the woman I was talking to wasn't all that familiar with Alicia's feet. Maybe she was just the person who answered the phone and had never even seen them. Maybe she wasn't good at describing things. But then I told myself that even if she *had* seen them, she still wouldn't have seen them through my eyes. This was subjective stuff; you couldn't take somebody else's word for it. I also reassured myself by thinking that anyone who advertised her feet in a sexual context must at least have some experience of the job in hand, must at least know what the issues are. You wouldn't say, 'Love me love my feet' if your feet were a

137

mass of corns and scar tissue. When I said I was still very interested I was given an address in St John's Wood, assured that anything I wanted to do was negotiable, and I said I'd be there within the hour.

I'd never been to a prostitute before. The thought had crossed my mind from time to time, in the way that it crosses your mind to try parachute jumping or to take saxophone lessons, but I had never been sure that I'd enjoy the experience. Now I was lost enough, reckless enough not to care.

I went to the address, a block of nineteen-fifties flats, one of those low-rise brick and stucco arrangements with lots of balconies and curved bay windows, and a jam of cars parked on the forecourt. Some men, Mike for instance, would no doubt have wanted sleaze and danger with their prostitution, but I was reassured that the block looked so smart and well cared for.

I rang one of a row of polished brass bells and a muffled, fuzzed female voice told me to come up to flat thirty-five on the third floor. I knew that I still had time to turn round and abort this little escapade. Meeting an unknown woman in a strange flat did not fill me with erotic expectation. Instead I could imagine myself being robbed, beaten up, humiliated. But so what? In Catherine's absence I felt robbed, beaten up, humiliated anyway. I would only be getting more of what I deserved. I carried on.

I reached the third floor, found flat thirty-five and knocked a little too hard on the door. It was immediately opened by a smart, dark-haired woman in a blue and pink track suit. She didn't look like my idea of a prostitute, more like an aerobics instructor or an assistant in a sports shop.

'Hello,' she said. 'I'm Alicia.'

I could tell at once from the voice that this was the

woman I'd spoken to on the phone. It appeared she was her own 'young lady'. As advertised, she had dark hair and large breasts, but personally I would not have mistaken her for a model. I looked down at her feet and saw that she was wearing a pair of high-heeled, gold court shoes, not the most perfect examples of fuck-me shoes you were ever going to come across but a reasonable attempt to show willing.

I could understand why she might wish to give the impression she was not simply a one-woman operation, and why she had talked about herself in the third person, but her reluctance and inability to describe Alicia's feet now appeared totally inexplicable. I must have looked confused and hesitant.

'Come in, love,' she said. 'Let's talk about what you have in mind, get the business side out of the way and then you can enjoy yourself.'

I was shown into the living room and she gave me a weak whisky and soda, and I sat down uneasily in a corduroy armchair. The flat was as empty and anonymous as a hotel room. There was no clutter, no personality, no suggestion that anybody lived here full-time.

There were other rooms in the flat, including, I supposed, the bedroom in which the physical side of our transaction would take place, but even though I heard and saw nothing, I got an uneasy feeling there was someone else in the flat somewhere; a pimp, or a minder, or maybe another prostitute.

'Right,' she said. 'Brass tacks. I don't do S and M of any kind, neither giving nor receiving. I'll walk on you if you like, but that's all. You can touch my feet if you want, kiss them, suck them, same with my toes and my shoes. You can massage them, rub them with creams, powders, oils and so on. Or I can massage you with them, either bare or in stockings or in white ankle socks. If you'd like a souvenir of the event I can provide a camera and film, though I would insist that my face doesn't appear in any of the photographs. Failing that I do have sets of prints available for purchase. I have a selection of boots, shoes and specialist footwear that I can wear at your discretion. Intercourse costs extra, oral costs a *lot* extra, and anal is out of the question. Right. What would you like?'

'I'd like to look at your feet,' I said.

She smiled affably enough and kicked off her gold shoes. I was prepared for something dramatic, feet that were either supremely beautiful or supremely disappointing, but in fact they were neither. There was certainly nothing bad or repellent about them. I would not have kicked them out of bed. They were feet I could quite happily fondle and kiss, but they were not feet that a man could lose his heart to. A man could not worship and adore them, could not become crazily obsessed with them. Essentially they were not Catherine's feet. And I suppose the bottom line was they were not feet that I wanted to waste a lot of money on.

From Alicia's menu I selected a small snack; a simple foot job. We negotiated that I would unzip my trousers and she would manipulate my cock with her bare feet. We agreed that a trip to the bedroom would not be necessary and she decided there was no need to remove her clothes.

Slightly to my surprise Alicia turned out to be highly skilled at her work. Her toes were strong and adept, her rhythm was vigorous and encouraging, and yet I didn't feel she was rushing me through the session. I was just starting to enjoy it when she suddenly stopped, reached into the pocket of her track suit, and in one continuous motion tore open a foil packet and unrolled a condom over my penis.

I was too surprised and baffled to object, and I'm sure my objections wouldn't have cut much ice, in any case. Besides, what would I have said? That a condom seemed a little excessive here, a little superfluous, a little insanely overcautious, that it appeared to be making a fetish out of 'safety'. I knew my opinions would not have been well received.

Alicia rapidly finished the job. She stood up and put her shoes back on. It was a touching gesture in a way. I mean, she could have slipped into something more comfortable, something tartan and fluffy perhaps. But I didn't get much time to admire the shoes. A couple of minutes later I was out of the flat, on the street, looking for the nearest pub. As I ordered myself a pint of lager I wondered if I should have bought some of the photographs she had for sale. They would have been a small but significant addition to the archive. A kind of first. Ah well, if I decided later that I really needed them I could go back for a return visit, but something told me my need was never going to be quite that great.

My session with Alicia was depressing enough but there were worse nights. It didn't look as though paying was going to work. Such transactions were bound to be brief and formal, and would leave far too much time to think about Catherine. So I went to bars and clubs and tried to pick up women. These women were not intended in any sense to replace Catherine but I hoped they might fill the dead time without her. It was surprisingly easy. I found plenty of women who were prepared to talk and drink and sleep with me. The fact that nothing relied on succeeding or failing with these women was somehow liberating. I wasn't too discriminating. I didn't much care who they were or what they looked like. I didn't even care what their *feet* looked like. I just took the women home, had sex with them, didn't bother to kiss their feet, didn't bother to photograph their shoes, didn't invite them down to see the archive. Christ, I was almost behaving like a normal person.

That was no good, so I decided to push my luck. I would get drunk and indifferent and reckless. I'd go up to a woman at the bar and start talking. 'Oh, hi there. Can I buy you a drink? Really nice shoes you're wearing. Really nice feet you have. Well, actually, it's the interaction of foot and shoe, of flesh and leather, nature and culture, art and artifice, the sweep of the foot, the curved architecture of the shoe, the pattern of veins and tendons below the surface of the skin, complex and intermeshed like tributary routes on a road map. I'd like to touch them, hold them, feel them on my face, on my tongue. I'd very much like to cover them in my sweat, my saliva, my semen . . .'

That use of the word semen always did it. That was the one word I found I couldn't say to a woman in a London bar. It always brought proceedings to a halt, like when I did my clipboard act and mentioned sex. In the confines of a nightspot, in a place where alcohol was sold, where sex was already on the agenda, it took a stronger word, a stronger image. But it also provoked a stronger reaction. I was sworn at, slapped, had drinks thrown at me. I didn't give a shit, but I learned my lesson. I stopped mentioning semen.

One night I found myself in the back of my car making inept attempts to have some sort of sex with a drunk, fleshy blonde. Her legs were splayed and bare. She'd kicked off her shoes and her feet were up on my shoulders. I turned my head and saw that these were not the feet of my dreams. They were plump and flat-footed and the silver pearl nail varnish was chipped and peeling. I was revolted, so revolted that I immediately took her fat little toes in my mouth and sucked each one in turn, disgusted, almost gagging, revelling in the self-abasement of it all. The woman didn't mind at all. She immediately appeared to be having a long and very satisfying orgasm.

Twenty-one

I've often wondered what it would have been like to have lived in China somewhere between the eleventh and the nineteenth centuries. This was a time when a whole population, a whole society, appears to have fallen victim to one very specific fetish: that of the bound foot. It wasn't a simple case of a few men and women getting together here and there and playing footsy. It was rather that for hundreds of years, millions of people decided that the female foot was the be all and end all of human sexuality. But not any old foot: only feet that were moulded and remodelled into a nightmarishly specific and rigid ideal – the lotus foot.

That was the name they gave to the anatomical curiosity that was created by foot binding. The big toe was left free, then the other toes and the body of the foot were strapped tight back, curving the foot and reducing its length, and also creating a sort of cleft on the underside between the end of the heel and the start of the sole. The flesh in this cleft became incredibly soft and sensitive. It was a brand new erogenous zone for the woman, and one into which the Chinese male loved to insert his penis.

There's some evidence that foot binding started with the Empress Taki. She was born in the eleventh century with tiny deformed feet, and as a mark of honour other women started binding their feet in imitation of her deformity. Now medieval Imperial China was no doubt a wacky place, but this simply doesn't sound like a credible example of human behaviour. In fact it sounds like deranged lunacy to me, but there's no doubt that it happened. Millions of women had their feet bound, and a great many of those who didn't probably wanted to.

I understand there was a considerable class element involved in foot binding. If you were a very rich woman you'd have your feet completely bound and therefore be completely crippled. If you were very poor you'd need to stand up in a field working all day in which case you couldn't afford to be bound at all. But in between there were lots of women who were only moderately rich, who might need to do a little work now and again, and so they were only moderately bound, only moderately crippled.

Of course, like any other good Westerner I find foot binding a complete horror. Crippling women isn't my idea of fun. And not least of the problems for a man like me is that the lotus foot doesn't look very appealing in a shoe. The foot itself is so distorted that it can never fit into an ordinary shoe at all. Such shoes as ever existed for women with bound feet were just loose slippers, shapeless in themselves.

But the main problem for me with the lotus foot is how it *looks*. I realize that beauty is always in the eye of the beholder, is indeed culturally specific, but the lotus foot seems to me to be quite objectively ugly. It looks like the foot of some strange, mutated animal, or some half-developed foetus. Call me an old square, but I can't see why someone would create, much less worship and have sex with, a thing that looked like that.

What exactly was going on here? Now, you might say that the people of China were attempting to redesign and customize the human body. And you might say that's what all clothes, all shoes, all fashion attempts to do. I'd know

145

what you meant, and I could sort of agree with you, but my gut feeling is that something very different is at stake. What I think was really going on in China for all those centuries was that these people had fallen in love with deformity for its own sake. They'd found a way to revel in ugliness. It can happen. I know.

In an ever more futile attempt to blot out Catherine, I went to a one-day conference at the ICA. Its title was 'Defeating the Object: the body as a medium of subversion.' There were lectures and workshops on tattooing and body piercing, on the feminist aesthetics of lesbian SM, and a good deal about 'the frenzy of the visible'.

Late in the afternoon I found myself in a seminar on fetishism. There were about twelve of us in the small white seminar room, more women than men, and a number of the women were wearing some serious FMs.

The first half-hour or so was spent discussing 'the female gaze' and how it differed from the male gaze. Then we debated whether or not women could be fetishists, and it came as no surprise, given the tenor of the group, when it was agreed that they could. They could be food fetishists, for instance, which sounded like no fun at all to me, and this led to a long and depressing discussion about eating disorders. It was said that shopping could be a form of fetishism, shoplifting too. Finally there was a debate about whether femininity itself wasn't perhaps a form of fetishism, and a couple of people suggested that femininity was a thing that could be put on and taken off in much the same way as a leather cat suit or a pair of thigh boots.

I wasn't really surprised that the discussion was on these terms. I'd hardly expected that we would regale each other with tales of our sexual escapades, much less have any fun. Nevertheless, I soon felt as though I was in a rapidly descending submarine and that all the oxygen around me was being used up. I didn't make any contribution to the seminar, and I wondered if I'd survive to the end of the session without screaming out in agony, but somehow I did.

It was late afternoon when we at last trooped out of the seminar room. The conference was over. Certain friendships and alliances had been established in the course of the day, and people were standing around in small groups continuing to talk and debate. I decided to head for the bar. I did not feel part of any group, nor had I struck up any friendships; nevertheless, when a young man walked up to me as though to start a conversation, I wasn't particularly surprised. He had been in the fetishism seminar, but he had contributed as little as I had.

He was in his early twenties, pale, wiry, nervous but studious looking. He was dressed all in black, with a black leather jacket, and he wore curious, high-tech spectacles. His hands and his Adam's apple looked too large for his body. His appearance seemed to hold the world at bay, but he was friendly enough when he talked to me.

'I don't think you enjoyed that seminar any more than I did,' he said.

'That depends how much you enjoyed it,' I said.

'It sucked.'

I didn't disagree.

'I'm not wholly against theory,' he continued. 'What I *am* against is people who need to hide *behind* theory. I mean, if people want to writhe around and suck each other's feet, why not just do it? Why do they feel they need to justify it intellectually?'

'I'll drink to that,' I said.

So we went to the bar and had a couple of bottles of beer

and we talked about (what else?) foot and shoe fetishism. He did far more talking than I did, but what he said made a lot of sense to me. I wondered what Mike would have made of it all. He'd have wanted both of us locked up, probably. I had no desire to describe my own practices and preferences to this stranger, no desire to tell him about Catherine, but he was happy enough to do most of the talking, and he continued ever more enthusiastically. He was now in a confessional mood, talking of the feet he had sucked, the shoes he had masturbated over, and so on. I was faintly embarrassed. He was assuming an intimacy that I neither desired nor intended to reciprocate, but I didn't try to stop him talking. I doubt whether I could have.

Before long I said I had to leave. He looked disappointed, as though he had much, much more to confess, but he said that he was going too. We left the bar, left the ICA and stood on the wide grass verge outside the entrance. Traffic swept up and down the road and I intended to say a swift, final goodbye to this stranger and hail a taxi. But he said, 'I don't live very far from here. I have a great deal of material you might be interested in.'

'What kind of material?' I asked.

'Photographs, drawings, books, samples. Some of it's very, very unusual. It's a kind of archive.'

That was enough for me. I took a chance. I agreed to go with him to his flat to view his material.

Although he called it a flat, it was little more than a bedsit, an attic room, up in the eaves of a peeling Victorian house. The walls of the room were painted black and it was furnished with junk-shop kitsch; an Elvis mirror, a lamp in the shape of a flying saucer, a piece of green fun fur thrown over the bed. It was far too small to contain anything that might truly be considered an archive, but there were a couple of filing cabinets and some metal lockers that he said contained his material.

He began by showing me his books. Some of them coincided with volumes in my own collection but there were all sorts of oddities here that I'd never seen before, and in many cases never wanted to see again. He had manuals of foot surgery and dissection, atlases of foot disease. He showed me pictures of hideously ugly feet, feet with burned skin, feet with frostbite, with toes missing, lepers' feet, and inevitably, endless pictures of feet that had been mutilated by foot binding. These obviously really hit the spot for him. He spent a long time leering over them and he obviously expected me to share his enthusiasm. I told him they revolted me, and he looked very disappointed, though it was clear he had plenty of other things that he thought would impress me.

He started to show me his shoe collection. He opened the metal lockers and pulled out samples. I was completely baffled. These were not FMs as I knew them. In fact they constituted the most dismal assembly of women's footwear I had ever seen. There were beige slingbacks, tasselled loafers, clogs, flip-flops, sneakers, plastic sandals. There were even Earth Shoes and Dr Scholls. In normal circumstances they would just have been ugly and aesthetically unpleasing, erotically neutral, but what made them actively disgusting was their condition. He had obviously gone to great lengths to find the most distressed, scuffed, worn-out examples of each type. Fabric was torn, soles and heels were loose or flapping, and the owners' feet had left them looking decayed, distorted, sweat laden.

I was horrified. The man disgusted me as much as his shoes did. I wanted to go.

149

'Now wait,' he said. 'Look at these. They're beauties, aren't they?'

By now I knew him well enough not to expect to share his sense of what constituted beauty and I was not at all surprised to find that he was waving a pair of unexciting, open-toed, black patent high heels. They were horribly grubby and cracked and extremely large. I looked at them indifferently and said nothing. And then, to my dismay and horror, I saw that he'd taken off his own shoes and socks and he slipped his bare feet into the black high-heeled shoes. He stood up and strutted across the room. His gait was a little wobbly, yet he looked as though he was well practised in wearing women's shoes. His feet looked totally, profoundly, disgustingly ugly, as ugly as anything I'd seen in his collection of pictures of bound and deformed feet.

I should probably have done nothing. I could have laughed at him or simply walked away, out of the building. But something in me couldn't leave it just like that, I was disgusted and outraged and angry. I admit that I was also a little surprised by the power of my own reaction. I wanted to preserve my dignity, to say something pithy and dismiss-ive and final, but words wouldn't come to me. Instead he was the one who spoke.

'I don't know what you're looking so mealy-mouthed about,' he said. 'I know you're into it every bit as much as I am.'

I didn't hit him exactly. I just headed for the door and as I went I pushed him out of the way. The flat of my hand made contact with his shoulder, nothing more violent than that, just a nudge really, and yet it resulted in him falling over. No doubt he wouldn't have fallen so easily had he not been wearing the high heels, nor would he have fallen quite so far. But he made no attempt to break his fall, didn't put out a hand or arm to stop himself, and his head hit the floor with a sharp, dry, full sound. He wasn't knocked out but his eyelids flickered and he looked about him as though he didn't recognize his surroundings or what had happened to him. He stared up at the ceiling for a moment, then slowly turned his head.

He had fallen in such a way that his head was next to the corner of the bed. I knelt down to make sure he was all right and I saw, hidden under the bed, a pair of spectacular silver and black FMs. I recognized the style immediately. I picked them up. Inside was Harold's familiar trade mark, the footprint and the lightning flash. I was doubly disgusted. This pathetic specimen on the floor had no right to own a pair of Harold's shoes. He didn't deserve them. He wasn't good enough. I grabbed the shoes and tried to stand up. The man protested groggily, and put out a hand to stop me. I was having none of that. I kicked him a few times in the ribs and then ran desperately out of his flat, taking Harold's shoes with me.

That was the night I went home and smashed the plaster casts of Catherine's feet. I didn't know why I was doing it. Perhaps it was indeed a symbolic act to try to free myself, but it really made no sense at all. I treasured those casts. They were all I had left of Catherine. In destroying them I was only hurting myself. And I realized then there was a part of me that might have been perfectly happy to destroy Catherine's actual feet as well as the casts. If they weren't going to be mine, then nobody else was going to have them, not even Catherine. And, as I sat there amidst the plaster debris, with the pair of silver and black shoes I'd stolen from the ICA man, I feared that I might be going insane.

Twenty-two

Given that pornography is a problem for just about every-body these days, it provides a special set of problems for the foot and shoe fetishist. There are, or at least there used to be, men who said they looked at *Playboy* simply for the articles. I suppose nobody needs to tell lies like that any more. But if I ever look at *Playboy* it's simply for the feet.

Now, I'm not made of stone. I'm not completely unmoved by the come-to-bed eyes and eagerly opened mouths of the women in girly magazines. I look at the long, smooth legs and the heavy, glossy breasts, and the silky buttocks and the hint or streak or flourish of inner pink, and, yes, sometimes I find that sexy. I'm not impervious to the erotic possibilities of stockings and suspenders, to strategically placed strands of leather or PVC or lace. But the only thing that really grabs me, the only thing I really care about is whether the model in the spread has a great pair of feet and a great pair of shoes.

You see surprisingly few bare feet in these pages. I suspect they aren't considered glamorous enough. The women therefore tend to wear high heels, and this ought to be a very good thing, yet there's often something tokenistic about it. The photographer or stylist thinks, Oh yeah, right, glamour shot, that means loads of make up, big hair, pair of high heels, without considering what constitutes good make up or good hair or good high heels. All too often the shoes are the wrong shape, the wrong colour, the wrong material. I'm not saying they always get it wrong, but they get it wrong more often than you might think possible.

However, even a casual browse through such magazines will reveal something very curious. It's extraordinary how often the photographs of the women are cropped in a way that leaves the feet out of the picture. Sometimes they will even be cropped so that some of the foot will be shown, but the toes will be outside the frame. More frustrating still, the woman will be on a four-poster bed or a *chaise-longue*, and some skein of exotic material will be wrapped around her, draped so as to show off her body, but her feet will be tangled up and concealed in the material.

I can think of two possible explanations for this. The first is that the photographers, or at least the layout artists, are so insensitive to the finer points of eroticism that they're not even *aware* that anyone could be interested in seeing women's feet. You might think it's unlikely. You might think anyone who makes a living in that world ought to be alive to these things but, let's face it, there are plenty of people in all sorts of jobs whose heart isn't in their work.

The other explanation is that there's something terribly wrong with the women's feet. Despite the beautifully made up face, the flatteringly lit skin, the improbably perfect body, the model's feet, I suppose, may be calloused, deformed, twisted, ugly as sin. By leaving them out of the shot, the photographer could be doing us a favour, and yet it's a favour I don't really need. I'd rather be allowed to make up my own mind about whether a given pair of feet are attractive or not.

Of course there are many rooms within the ruined mansion of pornography, but even when the imagery moves well outside the soft, 'girly' category, into the hard-core wing, my erotic concerns remain much the same. I see a porno mag or video, and in it the women may be servicing four or five people of their own or different sexes, they may be doing thrillingly obscene things with dildos, fists and bodily fluids, but I find I'm still looking to see what's going on below ankle level.

There are some specialist magazines for foot and shoe fetishists. I haven't seen that many of them, and I certainly haven't studied them, but the ones I've seen have been a considerable disappointment. They show feet being licked, toes being sucked, toes gripping cocks and probing vaginas, and these are all activities that in theory I find very appealing, but somehow, when you see a whole magazine devoted to them, it's too formulaic, too forced.

For all these reasons, pornography, whether hard or soft, often proves not to be an especially rich source of erotic imagery for the fetishist. *Vogue* is likely to offer classier, sexier, more elegant shoes than *Playboy* ever is. The models will probably be more beautiful, certainly they'll be more striking and better photographed. And quality of photography was something I was going to find out all about.

I will never know why I decided to break into Kramer's flat. It was a strange and very stupid thing to do, but then again, strange and very stupid behaviour had become something of a habit with me. I knew that I wanted to invade his territory, although I didn't quite know why I wanted that, and once I was inside I thought I would create a certain amount of wreckage, break a few precious things, smash a few major appliances. But perhaps I was also looking for something; clues maybe, a masochistic search for evidence about Catherine, proof of her closeness to him and her distance from me; stained sheets, love letters, something to reinforce my own pain and loss, to reinforce the sense of separation.

I went there in the evening, parked my car and waited until I saw Kramer leave his building at about nine o'clock. Then I went into action. I was deliberately reckless in smashing open his front door. There was nothing furtive or covert about it. I had armed myself with a large hammer and chisel, and I chopped away at the locks, used brute force on the hinges, and the door gave way. I found myself in a low, narrow passageway that ended in a flight of stairs. I turned on all the lights I could find. I wasn't going to skulk around in semi-darkness. I wanted to see what I had broken into. I went up the stairs, up another flight and another, to the top floor where there was a second locked door that needed opening, but now I felt like an old hand, and I cracked it open effortlessly.

I switched on more lights to see that I was in a sort of reception area, an outer office, with chairs, and a secretary's desk. There were notice-boards with invoices and business cards and Polaroids pinned to them, and a few composites from models and some contact sheets. There were framed photographs on the walls. It appeared that our man was in business as a photographer and that this place was a studio as well as a home. I saw my opportunities for havoc and damage expanding rapidly.

Beyond the reception area was a bathroom, a living room, a bedroom. I looked into these briefly but the studio was my real destination, the place where he took his photographs, where the expensive equipment was. I found it easily; a high wide space. The roof and one of the walls were glass but there were drapes and blinds everywhere, some black, some white, absorbing or reflecting light, lining and sub-dividing the space.

155

Reflectors and spot lamps and flash units were clamped to a framework of stands and gantries, and a big plate camera stood centre stage, focused on a bare paper roll of backdrop. I shoved the camera with both hands and it fell with a satisfyingly heavy thud, though there was no sound of breakage.

There were lots of storage units around the place, filing cabinets, box files, plan chests, boxes of negatives and contact sheets. I ripped open a few. They were dull stuff, portraits of smiling business executives, shots of hairdriers and shampoo bottles. As I lost interest in them I dropped them on to the floor.

And then I opened the plan chest. It contained finished prints, huge, shiny, hard-edged photographs, sixteen by twenty or bigger, giant enlargements. I flipped through some of them, looking at the magnified faces and products and rapidly cast them aside. They were of no interest either. I was about to close the chest when I saw another set of prints, carefully wrapped up in paper. I pulled some of them out, unwrapped them, and stopped stone dead.

I could barely believe it but they were blow ups of Catherine's feet, many, many times larger than life, showing and highlighting every detail, every flawless feature, the sheen and grain of the skin, the curvature of the nails, the thin, precise lines of cuticle, the traces of musculature and blood vessels.

I pulled the rest of the photographs out of the drawer, twenty, maybe thirty, portraits of Catherine's bare feet, sometimes stretching and pointing, sometimes on tiptoe, sometimes at rest, photographs taken from subtly different angles, with different gradations of illumination and shadow, different degrees of contrast. The quality of the prints, the professionalism of the photography was overwhelming. It made all the examples in my archive look tacky and inept. I was devastated. I felt utterly hopeless and defeated. Until then it had been possible to tell myself that nobody could care for Catherine in quite the way I did, that nobody else could appreciate and worship her feet as I could. Yet here was evidence that Kramer, this stranger, this unknown quantity, this man she had been able to find so quickly after separating from me, was every bit as obsessional and fetishistic as I was.

I stood and stared at the black and white photographs; but monochrome, eloquent though it was, only told half the story. I somehow knew there would be more. I knew there would be colour images as well. I threw open a few metal cupboards until I came across boxes of transparencies. Ham-fisted and over-eager, I yanked out handfuls of slides, shuffled them, tossed them aside until I found what I was looking for.

There were at least a hundred of them, large format slides of Catherine's bare feet. I held them up to the light but that was too frustrating. They were too small, the illumination wasn't good enough. I intended to take some away with me and I immediately stashed a few in my pockets, but that still wasn't enough. I was raging with adrenalin, flapping with recklessness. I decided I wanted to see them here and now on the big screen. I decided to have myself a little slide show.

I found a projector and set it up where the plate camera had been, so that it would project on to the studio's paper backdrop. I loaded the magazine and slipped it in, turned off the lights, took the remote control in my fist and settled down for showtime. Catherine's feet appeared in front of me, ten, twelve feet high, seen against different backgrounds, strong saturated purples and reds, but also on swathes of fur, on slick, smooth rubber, on a studded black leather jacket. And whereas her nails had been unpainted in the black and white prints, here they were lacquered a smooth, thick cerise.

Of course, I did wonder how come Catherine's feet were bare in all the shots, how come Kramer hadn't photographed her in shoes, but I could only think that his tastes weren't exactly the same as mine. He apparently went for nature unadorned.

I stood there in the darkness, dust following currents through the beam of light, my eyes fixed on the projected images, Catherine's feet filling my entire field of vision. I was transported and I was stiff as a poker. My heart was drumming, my head was full of blood and interference, and that was when Kramer returned.

Maybe he'd forgotten something, or maybe I'd miscalculated and he'd only slipped out to buy cigarettes. I didn't hear him enter the room behind me; the noise of the projector fan was loud enough to cover the sound and, let's face it, my concentration was elsewhere. Suddenly a light was switched on and the image on the screen was bleached to a thin, pale version of itself. I dropped the remote control and turned round to see Kramer staring at me.

'What the fuck?' he said to himself.

He was angry but I could see he was also frightened. He'd caught an intruder in his home and these days nobody knows what a cornered intruder might do to you. I could see him looking around the room, at the small pockets of disorder I'd caused, but it was plain that I hadn't just trashed the place, that I wasn't simply a wrecker or burglar. He picked up a heavy tripod, as much to defend himself as to attack me, but then he gave me a good looking over, noticed the image being projected, and I could see something shifting behind his eyes, something falling into place.

'I think I know who you are,' he said. 'I think I've heard all about you.'

'No,' I said. 'You don't know me.'

'I think I do,' he insisted, and he immediately came at me. Suddenly he regarded me as no threat whatsoever, and he hit me in the stomach with the end of the tripod. It was a good shot. I was winded, in pain, and my legs felt as though the bones in them had turned to mercury. I swayed, teetered, fell on my side. Kramer stood over me. He could have hit or kicked me anywhere he wanted to, a free hit. He could have crippled me probably, but instead he pushed me over on to my back and put his foot on my neck and pressed. He was wearing heavy, thick-soled work boots, and the pattern of tread was cold against my windpipe. Experimentally, he increased and decreased the pressure of his foot, as though he was revving an accelerator. I didn't struggle or cry out. I just watched him and tried to breathe through my nose.

'You're a real comedy act, aren't you?' he said, and he took his foot off me. Automatically my hand went up to rub my throat but he kicked it away. I lay still after that. I could see he was trying to come up with another way of hurting me. At last he looked satisfied; he'd thought of something. He brought the sole of his right boot down on to my face, flattening my nose, its threatening pressure spread evenly between my forehead and my mouth. But he didn't put all his weight on it, that wasn't his game, not yet.

'Now lick it,' he said. 'Lick it clean.'

I still had some pride. 'Fuck you,' I said, and then he raised his foot to about knee height and stamped on my face. Something light, brittle and very well supplied with pain receptors and blood seemed to snap behind my nose and it became difficult to breathe.

'Get up,' he said. 'Get up. You want to see slides, I'll show you some slides.'

He dragged me up by the hair and threw me down on to a couch. He went to a storage cabinet, pulled out a box of transparencies and loaded them into the projector.

'See how you like these,' he said.

A new set of images filled the makeshift screen. They were of Catherine but they were no longer just of her feet. They were of her whole body, naked and not alone. Kramer was in the photographs too, equally naked. I was being shown images of the two of them having sex. They were explicit shots, pornographic, I suppose. They made no attempt to be art, and neither were they posed exactly. I could see in the pictures that Kramer was holding a cable release and he was obviously pressing it and firing the shutter as and when he moved into a position that appealed to him, that seemed photogenic.

I didn't want to watch, but it was hard to look away. The transparencies changed rapidly as Catherine and Kramer changed position, changed places: and, precisely as if I was looking at a pornographic magazine, I found it strangely easy to blot out the images of limbs and bodies, faces and genitals, and focus simply on Catherine's feet. They were as magnificent as ever. I felt terrible about it but I soon found myself getting aroused again. I couldn't face it. I stood up and confronted Kramer. 'This is stupid,' I said. 'You've got Catherine. You've humiliated me. Isn't that enough for you?'

I think more than anything else that must have surprised and confused him. He moved as though to threaten me again, but he was half-hearted about it now. I'd had enough

160

and I felt that he had too. I walked away, turning my back on him. I knew there was a possibility he might hit me from behind, but I calculated that he wouldn't. I left the studio, left the building, convinced myself that he wasn't following me, and went back to my car.

I felt my face, tried to look at it in the rear-view mirror. It was wet with blood and dirt but nothing felt as if it was broken. I knew I was lucky. I could have been beaten to a pulp or I could have been handed over to the police as a burglar. I had good reason to feel relieved, but in fact I felt ashamed, disgusted, and I also felt truly sorry for myself. I needed a bit of sympathy so I headed for the only place where I thought I had any conceivable hopes of receiving a welcome: Harold Wilmer's shop.

Twenty-three

Harold's shop was locked up, and there were no lights on inside. The window looked strangely empty as though he had given up trying to attract custom. However, there were lights on in his flat upstairs. I pressed the doorbell but at first there was no answer; perhaps Harold was used to passing drunks ringing it in the middle of the night. But I persisted, made it plain that I wasn't going away, and eventually a curtain was pulled back and Harold's face appeared. He looked down at me, neither surprised nor pleased to see me, having no sense of urgency nor of my need. It took him a long time to shamble down the stairs and open the door.

'Yes?' he said, as though he was confronting a man peddling religious tracts, but then he saw the blood on my face and my wounded looks and he let me in.

'I'm sorry to arrive like this,' I said. 'I didn't have anywhere else to go.'

I had never been inside Harold's flat before and I imagined it would be some dark labyrinth of a place. In the event it was just a small, old man's flat, full of big heavy furniture that he had to squeeze past or climb over in order to move around the room. There was a carpet that might not have been vacuumed in years, and dust was spread thickly and evenly over every horizontal surface. But there was nothing particularly odd or eccentric about any of it, and there was no display of his handiwork, no covert stash of exotic shoes.

However, two things caught my eye. First, I noticed a framed photograph that sat on the mantelpiece above the hissing gas fire. It was a snapshot of a plump-cheeked, open-faced young woman. Harold saw me looking and said, 'Yes, that's Ruth.'

I was surprised. She was not as I'd imagined her and she did not look like anybody's idea of a prostitute. It was hard to believe that the wholesome-looking woman in the photograph had strutted through alien bedrooms, touching strangers, being paid for sex, wearing shoes Harold had made for her. Her face looked neither sexual nor knowing, but perhaps there were other faces that she kept for professional purposes.

The other thing that leapt out at me was a cast of Catherine's right foot that rested on the sideboard in the yellow glow of a table lamp. It was marked with grubby fingerprints, and I wondered what use Harold had for it and what had happened to the other one.

I sat down in a furrowed armchair and continued to feel sorry for myself while Harold poured me a small brandy and fetched a damp cloth to wipe the mess off my face.

'What happened to you?' Harold asked as he too sat down, but he didn't sound very interested.

'It's a long story,' I said, and with some guilt I described my bad times with Alicia, with my ugly-footed women, with the man from the ICA. Most shameful of all, I admitted that I had smashed the plaster casts of Catherine's feet. Harold listened and I confessed. I wanted him to be shocked and disapproving. I wanted him to tell me how stupid and wrong I'd been, but he wouldn't give me that satisfaction. He just nodded from time to time, as though everything I was confessing to was par for the course. But so far I'd said nothing about my encounter with Kramer.

'I feel such a fraud compared to you, Harold,' I said. 'I feel that my behaviour isn't justified. I shouldn't be going off the rails like this. I mean, all that's happened is I've been dumped by my girlfriend, whereas you . . .'

I couldn't finish my sentence. Harold looked as though his features had been set in cement. I wasn't telling him anything he didn't already know.

'None of this explains the blood on your face,' he said.

So I told him all about Kramer, about my break-in, about the pictures of Catherine's feet and, for the first time, he seemed to get interested.

'That's a strange one, isn't it,' he said. 'That he's as obsessed with Catherine's feet as you are. I wonder why. I wonder if she sought him out deliberately. Maybe you've given her a taste for it.'

'Am I supposed to feel good about that?'

'No, I suppose not.'

I took the few transparencies I'd slipped into my pockets and showed them to Harold. He held them up to the light, peered closely, but didn't seem very impressed.

'Do you think he's called the police?' Harold asked.

'No, I don't think so.'

'But he knows who you are.'

'Apparently.'

'He'll tell Catherine, no doubt.'

'I guess so.'

'This is no way to get her back, is it?' said Harold sadly.

'No,' I agreed.

'So what are you going to do now?'

'Sit here for a while. Go home. Get drunk. Get some sleep.'

'I mean, what are you going to do about Kramer?'

'What can I do? It's over with. I probably got what I deserved.'

Harold gave a strange little laugh, somewhat like a hiccup, somewhat like a whoop of delight. 'How about getting some revenge?' he said.

'Like what?'

He reached over and picked up the photograph of Ruth and stared at it, as though he was looking right through it, peering into another world.

He said, 'You know, above all else, beyond all the other feelings I have, I'm chiefly very *angry* about Ruth's death. Still. Perhaps more now than ever. And for a long time I tried to focus that anger. I wanted her death to be somebody's fault. And it might have been possible to blame the doctors, or our polluted environment, or even to blame God, but in reality Ruth died of what we have to call natural causes, and being angry with nature is as absurd as it is futile.

'I used to wish that a drunken driver had killed her, or a sex murderer, maybe one of her clients, because then there would have been someone to blame, someone to be angry with, someone to take revenge on. And I'm absolutely sure I'd have taken that revenge. I'd very happily have killed Ruth's killer.'

He was as cold and as serious as I had ever seen him. He undoubtedly believed what he was saying but I wasn't at all sure that *I* did. I've no doubt that most of us are capable of murder in certain specific circumstances, but it was still impossible to think of mild little Harold Wilmer as any sort of killer.

'I'm sorry,' I said apologetically. 'I know my loss can't possibly be in the same league as yours.'

'Not true,' he replied. 'For you things are actually much harder. You're angry because Catherine's gone. You want her back but you're angry with her. She's both the cause and the object of your anger. You're so angry with her you could kill her, but if you killed her you wouldn't have her at all and could never have her again. I can see it's a difficult situation.'

'Hey, steady on, Harold. I haven't the slightest urge to kill Catherine.'

'No? But you do need a focus for all that anger, don't you? I always said you did. And Kramer fits the bill nicely.'

It made some sort of sense.

'OK,' I said. 'You could be right. Maybe that's why I broke into his place, because I was angry and wanted to destroy something.'

'But you found the photographs of Catherine's feet and that made you angrier still, I'd guess.'

I wasn't sure that they'd made me angry exactly, and sitting there in Harold's armchair, I didn't feel angry at all. I felt lost, pathetic, trivial. I didn't say that to Harold. It would have been letting him down. If he wanted to play at being an amateur psychologist, if he wanted to think I was trying to come to terms with my anger, I had no urge to argue.

'But,' said Harold, 'then Kramer caught you and humiliated you. At this very moment, you probably feel as though you want to kill Kramer.'

'No,' I protested again. 'I don't have the slightest urge to kill Kramer, either.'

Harold was starting to worry me. I'd never seen him like this. These casual, literal references to killing weren't in character with the man I thought I knew. He looked at the photograph of Ruth again, then at me. I felt he was trying to see what I was made of, whether I was quality merchandise, whether I was good enough for whatever he had in mind. I knew I wasn't.

'No, perhaps you couldn't kill Kramer,' he conceded. 'But I could.'

Later that night he did.

Twenty-four

It was only a small item in the newspaper, the 'In Brief' column, hemmed in between an arson attack on a school for the blind and a paragraph about two road builders who'd raped a male hitchhiker. It said,

> Mr Robert Kramer, a professional photographer, was found dead in his studio by cleaners this morning. Police say they are keeping an open mind about the cause of death and are anxious to interview friends and colleagues.

Horror and disbelief tumbled over each other in me. I read the item again. It wasn't enough. I wanted details, a full report, descriptions of the body and the scene of the crime, all the available data about the time and means of death. I wanted to know what goes through a policeman's 'open mind'.

I didn't want to believe it had anything to do with Harold. I hoped it was just a dreadful coincidence, and yet, given the way he'd talked that night, it was all too easy to believe it. I phoned his shop. It was a long time before he answered.

'Kramer's dead,' I blurted.

'Who?' said Harold.

'Come on, Harold, you know what I'm talking about.'

'I don't think I do,' he said.

It occurred to me that maybe the police were already

there, that they were listening in on the conversation, hence his reticence.

'Is there somebody there?' I asked.

'Nobody here but me.'

'Harold, what do you know about Kramer?'

'I know nothing about anyone of that name.'

'What are you playing at, Harold? I can't believe you're acting like this. Were you there? Did you . . . ?'

I couldn't bring myself to ask directly whether Harold had committed a murder. Some ludicrous sense of propriety was still in place.

'I really don't know what you're talking about,' Harold replied.

'I don't want to believe you did it,' I said.

'Nobody's asking you to,' Harold said flatly. 'How could anyone think I killed a man I've neither met nor heard of.'

'What are you saying, Harold?'

'It might be better if we didn't talk for a while,' he said. 'Not that we've had much in common since Catherine stopped seeing you.'

That was when I truly realized that Catherine's absence meant as much to Harold as it did to me. If Harold had killed Kramer, and I still hoped to God that he hadn't, he might like to pretend he'd done it as a favour to me, but it appeared now that he had pressing reasons of his own. It seemed to me that Kramer had taken Catherine away from Harold just as surely as he'd taken her away from me.

'I'll be going away for a little while,' Harold continued. 'Doing a bit of travelling. Going abroad.'

'That's as good as admitting that you did it,' I said.

'Not quite.'

'Where are you going?'

'It's probably better if you don't know that.'

169

'What if I need to contact you?'

'You'll have no reason to contact me.'

'I should go to the police about this,' I said.

'I think that wouldn't be very clever of you,' said Harold. 'What would you tell them? That Harold Wilmer, a sad old shoemaker, got it into his head to kill a man? They'll ask how you know, and you'll have to tell them you were there, that the man stole your girlfriend, that you broke into his flat, that you had a fight. Not very clever at all.'

'Harold, I can't believe this.'

'You don't need to believe anything. All right? Just get on with your life, as I intend to. I'm going now. Good-bye.'

He put the phone down on me and when I immediately called back the line rang without being answered. I ran out of my house, into my car and drove to the shop. It wasn't a quick drive at the best of times and the traffic was terrible. By the time I got there I wasn't at all surprised to find that he'd gone. The shop was empty and locked. I pounded on the door until a couple of passers-by stopped and asked me what I wanted. I said nothing. I got in my car, put my foot down and drove. I didn't know where I was going. Maybe I was heading for Heathrow, maybe I was driving around in the hope of seeing Harold wandering the streets, or in a taxi, making his getaway, leaving the scene of the crime, but it wasn't long before I abandoned that absurd enterprise. Harold had gone. Harold Wilmer, the mild-mannered, murderous shoemaker, had done a very successful disappearing act.

Over the next couple of weeks I spent a lot of time combing the newspapers, looking for some follow-up piece, a report on the inquest, an announcement that a full-scale murder investigation had started, or alternatively that

Kramer's death had been declared an accident or suicide. But I found nothing. What was I to do? I couldn't call the police and ask how they were getting on. All I could do was try to get on with my life and hope that no news was good news.

Of course, I tried to phone Catherine. It seemed to me that her command not to phone her meant nothing now that Kramer was dead. Not that it mattered anyway. I phoned but there was only the sound of a disconnected line. I went to her flat and got no reply on her bell, so I pressed a lot of the others, pretending I was the postman. People are very gullible. I eventually spoke through the entryphone to a neighbour, a trusting old lady, who told me that Catherine had moved out. I asked how long ago. Oh, maybe a couple of weeks. Had she left a forwarding address? No, but the neighbour had a feeling she might have gone back to America. Where, I asked. What city? What state? Could she even tell me north, south, east, or west? By now the neighbour had worked out that I wasn't really the postman and put down her phone.

I was frustrated but I saw how it might be for the best. If Catherine had really left a couple of weeks ago then perhaps she wasn't even aware that Kramer was dead. I don't know why that pleased me so much.

I did find it strange that Catherine and Harold should both disappear at the same time, and for the briefest moment it occurred to me that they might possibly have gone away together. But, no, that made no sense at all. It had to be nothing more than coincidence.

Kramer's death straightened me out a lot. I no longer wallowed in the misery of Catherine's departure. Neither did I go around visiting prostitutes, picking up women, going to seminars on fetishism. I did my very best to lead a quiet, blameless life. It was dull stuff. It would have been nice to meet up with Mike and Natasha, but I was staying out of that one for the moment. Of course, I still had my archive and that remained a source of occasional pleasure, but whereas it had been a fluid, growing collection it now became fixed and static. I thought it safest not to add to it; no more interviewing in the street, no more snatched photographs, no more stolen shoes. I was trying not to act suspiciously. I was acting like a criminal, albeit a reformed one.

I was still occasionally tempted to go to the police. Yes, I would have had to confess to the break-in and to the fight with Kramer, but wouldn't the mere fact of making a confession prove that I wasn't the murderer? Well no, I could see that was a game of double and triple bluff, and would prove nothing. But wouldn't my sheer innocence stand out? Surely the police would be able to tell I wasn't the murderous type. But no, I didn't believe that either. Innocent people are sometimes found guilty. People go to jail on the basis of far skimpier evidence than that against me. The chances of them catching Harold, believing and proving that he was the real killer, seemed slim. If the police were looking for a convenient hook on which to hang this murder I'd do just fine.

Then, one night, a stranger came to my door and I knew straight away he was police. In a curious way I was relieved. I knew it had to happen sooner or later. He was young and big, his blond hair was cropped to a post-harvest stubble and his clothes were too tight round his arms and thighs. The pint had been forced into a grey double-breasted half-pint suit.

'I wonder if I can waste a couple of minutes of your time,' he said in a surprisingly easy tone.

'I am sort of busy,' I replied, only too willing to put him off if he could be put off that easily.

But then he flashed his badge and looked as though he meant business. I didn't hear what rank he was, not that it would have meant anything to me, but I caught the name Crawford and it was obvious that he was going to come in, invited or not.

'This won't take long,' he said as he clumsily pushed past me into the hall. 'Don't worry. It's about someone and something you probably don't know anything about.'

For a moment I thought perhaps this visit had nothing at all to do with Kramer, that perhaps it was about stolen cars or the local neighbourhood watch. We walked into the living room and he sat down on the sofa, sprawled a little and blatantly looked round.

'You live on your own, sir?'

'Yes.'

'I knew it. You can always tell. It's something to do with the room lacking a woman's touch. You ever been married?'

'No.'

'But you've got a girlfriend?'

'Not at the moment, no.'

I must have sounded overdefensive, though what was I defending myself against? Unspecified charges of sexual inadequacy? He saw me looking troubled and he slapped on a tight smile and waved a hand as if to say not to worry, it was all right by him, that wasn't what he was here for, though he didn't altogether convince me. He resumed his inspection of my décor.

'It doesn't look like a queer's room either.'

'Well, it wouldn't,' I said.

'No. I know that you do have girlfriends. I know that you went out with Catherine for instance.'

'You're well informed,' I said.

'Not as well as I'd like to be. Anyway, you and Catherine didn't last very long. Right?'

Things were happening too fast. Nothing was quite sinking in. I wanted to ask him who'd told him about me and Catherine, and whether he knew where she was, how I could get in contact with her, but that would have sounded desperate. I was too busy thinking this through to answer his question, but he waited for me.

'Didn't last long,' he repeated.

'Not long enough, no,' I said.

'Well, length isn't everything.'

It felt like he was testing me. Was I the kind of man who laughed at oblique jokes about penis length? On this occasion I wasn't. I pretended not to realize that he was joking, so he gave a laugh that was long, loud and dirty enough for both of us.

'Would you describe it as a casual relationship?' he asked when he'd finished laughing.

'No, I wouldn't.'

'So it was a short-lived but intense affair?'

'If you like, yes. Look, is this about Catherine? You said it was about someone I probably didn't know.'

'I'm gathering background, all right? So why did you split up?'

'Is this really relevant?'

'Obviously,' he said. 'I wouldn't be arsing around asking you irrelevant questions, would I, sir? Why did you split up?'

'You'd have to ask her. It wasn't my decision.'

'We would if we knew where she was, but we don't, and I assume you don't either.'

'That's right,' I said, and at that moment I was extremely

glad I didn't know. Having to tell this man her whereabouts would have been an act of terrible betrayal.

'You don't mind helping me like this, do you?' he asked abruptly.

'No, but if it's about Catherine . . .'

'It's about someone called Robert Kramer. He was Catherine's bloke after you. Your replacement.'

'Is he in trouble?' I asked, hoping I didn't sound quite as transparent as I felt.

'Well, he's dead, isn't he? No trouble for him, quite a lot of trouble for me. I'm surprised you didn't see it in the paper.'

'Why should I? But, I mean, that's terrible, his death.'

'So you didn't know him?'

'No.'

'Ever see him? Speak to him? Tell him to get his hands off your woman?'

'Not really my style,' I said truthfully enough.

'Come on,' he urged. 'You see your bird walking down the street on the arm of some new bloke, this bird who you've had a short, intense relationship with that you didn't want to end. Well, it'd be pretty unnatural not to feel angry and pissed off about it, not to want to stick one on the little fucker, wouldn't it?'

'I felt things, but I didn't feel like sticking one on him, no.'

'Didn't feel like killing him?'

'Are you serious?'

'Not really, no. You don't look the type. But I was wondering if you knew anything about Mr Kramer's sexual proclivities.'

'Why would I?' I answered.

'You might know through Catherine. I was thinking that

175

maybe all three of you had some sexual proclivities in common.'

'What are you saying?'

'I'm not saying anything,' he said. 'I'm just asking some routine questions.'

None of it sounded even remotely routine to me, but I said simply, 'No, I don't know anything about Kramer's sexual proclivities.'

'So you can't be any help to us with his murder?'

'His murder?' I said slowly and deliberately, feigning shock and surprise, and hoping I wasn't overdoing it. 'You never said he was murdered.'

'That's true,' Crawford agreed. 'And you probably can't tell us anything about the mutilation either.'

'Jesus. What mutilation?' This time the shock was real and I hoped it didn't betray the inauthenticity of my previous reaction.

'We don't release that sort of stuff to the papers,' Crawford said, like he was letting me in on a trick of the trade. 'If you do, then you get a spate of copycat incidents. That's amazing, isn't it? Most murderers are so fucking unoriginal they can't even think up their own way of killing someone. But put it in the papers that somebody's going around chopping people's heads off with a chain saw and they're all at it.'

'Somebody used a chain saw on this man Kramer?'

'No. That's just a for instance. I can't tell you what form or forms of mutilation are involved, not that I think you're likely to commit a copycat murder.'

By now I was well beyond being able to hide my reactions. It was bad enough to think that Harold had committed the murder, but mutilation was a whole new horror. I was sure that my face and body were sending all kinds of quisling signals about what I was really thinking and feeling. Then Crawford said, 'So you didn't do it, then? The murder.'

I was so taken by surprise that I had no time to consider my response. I just said, 'Don't be stupid.'

'I'm not stupid,' he replied, and in that simple phrase he conveyed a whole world of strength and anger and violence. He was warning me not to mess with him, not to take him for a fool, not to cross him. I felt like apologizing. Then he said, 'How would it be if I sent a couple of lads to search this place?'

'What for?' I asked.

'For clues, that sort of thing. How would you feel?'

'Well, I'd object, frankly.'

'Good,' he said, putting a tick on some mental list. 'I like that. Most ordinary, innocent people *would* object. If you'd told me to go ahead, that you had nothing to hide, then I'd have been very suspicious.'

I took some small satisfaction from knowing that I was behaving like an ordinary, innocent person, though that was not what I felt like.

'Because, I mean,' he continued, 'everybody's got something to hide, haven't they? It might be a few porn videos or a secret diary or some ladies' underwear. We've all got that certain little something, haven't we?'

'Well, yes, I suppose, I mean, no, not really, not in my case.'

'There's no need to be shy with me,' Crawford said. 'I've heard it all. And I've seen most of it. And as long as nobody gets hurt and as long as kids and drugs and animals aren't involved, then who really cares? Some people want to drink each other's piss, some want to shove their fists up each other's backsides. There are blokes out there who like to

177

have their foreskins nailed to the floorboards. Now you and I might think they're sick, filthy sods who should be taken outside and given a good kicking, but, anyway, it's a free country, isn't it?'

I was so lost by now, so far out of my depth, so in need of time to collect my thoughts, so confused about what this man was saying, even more confused about what he actually meant, so unsure of what he wanted from me, that I could barely keep up with him. But now he was being nice to me again.

'I can see you're a decent bloke,' he said. 'I can see you're not into all that weird stuff. But what about this Kramer? What was he into, eh?'

'I've told you, I've no way of knowing.'

'Not true,' he said. 'You know Catherine. You know what kind of thing she might go for. Do you think she'd go for something a bit kinky and dangerous?'

'You'll have to ask her,' I said.

'I'm asking you, cunt.'

All the aggression was there again, all the threats and veiled intentions. I was scared. I said, 'Well, I don't know, maybe. Yes, sometimes Catherine could be a bit . . . wild.'

I didn't think that answer was going to satisfy him but he unexpectedly stood up and headed for the door.

'Correct answer,' he said, and suddenly he looked pleased, both with me and himself. 'You know crime's a strange thing. There are very few people who commit just one crime. In general one crime leads on inexorably to the next, like joining up the dots until the final picture appears.'

I must have been looking particularly blank, since he tried another way to make me understand.

'Look at it like this, a man who commits armed raids on a post office isn't too worried about having a TV licence or

178

getting his car insured. You can be sure that the man who killed Kramer has committed other crimes too.'

This sounded like rubbish to me. As far as I knew, which was not far, Harold hadn't ever committed any other crime.

'Does that mean you're looking for a man who hasn't paid his TV licence?'

I wasn't trying to be glib or tough, it just came out that way. Crawford had to think before he decided whether or not to be angry or insulted.

'One more thing before I go. Have you got a pen and paper? I want to show you something.'

I handed him a piece of paper and a ballpoint and he drew the outline of a footprint with a lightning flash through it.

'Any idea what that means?' he asked.

'No,' I said.

'No, I didn't think you would have. Well, that's all right then. I'll be on my way, but take care. I'll be in touch.'

I was shaking by the time he left and he must have seen that. I hadn't a clue what the session had really been about. He could hardly think I'd killed Kramer, otherwise he wouldn't have been so easy on me. But I had been so thrown by his questions and his presence that he must surely have worked out that I knew more than I was telling. He obviously knew more than he was telling too, and I'd have given a lot to find out what. The fact that he hadn't managed to talk to Catherine seemed to be infinitely in my favour.

But I was worried by his notions of criminal psychology. As far as I was concerned foot fetishism didn't come into the same category as urolagnia, fisting and having your foreskin nailed to the floor, but I suspected Crawford saw things differently. Foot fetishism did indeed seem to be something that Catherine, Kramer and I had in common, but was that supposed to suggest that we had murder in common too? And why had he shown me the drawing of the footprint with a flash through it? That must mean he had some inkling of Harold's involvement. Why hadn't he said so?

Crawford scared me. He struck me as devious, vicious and not nearly as bright as he wanted to appear; a lethal combination. But how bright would he need to be to pin the murder on me? Making a clean breast of it seemed like even less of an option. I was on my own. I was the only suspect, the only witness and there was nobody in the whole world who was going to do anything to help me. I found that knowledge strangely invigorating.

Twenty-five

I made a big decision. I hired a white van. I'd already amassed a small city of cardboard boxes, all marked with the names of washing powders and potato snacks, and these poor things were going to become the containers of a lifetime's erotic obsession. I was loading up my archive, moving it out of my cellar.

I felt I was attempting to get rid of evidence, but evidence of what? Certainly nothing to do with murder, as far as I could see. I was simply trying to cover up a large chunk of my personality in case Crawford changed his mind and decided to search my house after all.

In the beginning I thought all that was needed was a gentle pruning of the archive, a shedding of the most 'incriminating' material. It was obviously going to be necessary to get rid of the slides of Catherine's feet, the ones I'd stolen from Kramer's studio. They, as far as I knew, were the only direct link between me and the dead man, so of course they had to go. But it also seemed sensible to get rid of any other pictures of Catherine's feet, the ones I'd taken myself, because that looked like something I had in common with Kramer. For much the same reason, I thought I'd better be rid of all the other foot pictures I'd taken, the ones of my old girlfriends, and the ones I'd taken with my hidden camera.

Then it was only common sense to move out all the shoes I'd stolen over the years. If nothing else, they showed I was a criminal, albeit of a very specialized and comparatively harmless kind, or so it seemed to me, but I didn't want to give Crawford anything he could possibly use against me. I kept recalling his absurd logic; that a man who committed murder would have committed some other trivial crimes first, that a minor aberration was a major pointer, a giant neon arrow, towards some bigger, more serious aberration. He might well think that if I'd stolen shoes and broken into Kramer's flat I could be capable of anything.

Then, painful though it was, I knew I had to get rid of the shoes that Harold had made for Catherine. It broke my heart to do it, but they all contained the trade mark of footprint and lightning flash, and their existence in my basement proved that I'd lied to Crawford about not recognizing the symbol. That left the archive with a very impoverished set of women's footwear. It was as though all the best specimens had been looted. I could have hung on to what remained, but in Crawford's eyes their possession might still have been evidence of sexual variance, so I felt they had to go too.

I was trying desperately to see myself as someone else might, not as a normal, healthy man with an intense, but entirely sane sexual preference, but as some dodgy pervert, a thief and a liar, or in Crawford's terms, a murderer in the making. In this process of externalization, I could see that wandering the streets asking women about their sex lives mightn't be seen as simple harmless fun either, so I decided that all the questionnaires had better go too.

The cuttings and printed material might have stayed, I suppose, but there were more problems there. Many of the books, for instance, dealt with the psychopathology of fetishism, and I didn't want anything around the place suggesting that I was a psychopath. And as for my scrapbooks, well, I could see that certain people might think they were pretty strange. A lot of the pictures in there didn't show complete women. In many cases I'd, so to speak, cut them in pieces. I'd kept the feet and thrown away the rest. I could now see how this might be construed as a form of mutilation. So they went as well. In fact, in the end, gradually and reluctantly, but inevitably, I decided it all had to go, the whole archive, the whole shebang. Once the cream had gone what was the point trying to live with the thin, skimmed remains? But go where?

To have been absolutely safe I should probably have burned the lot, made a bonfire, a sacrifice, a funeral pyre, and to be fully correct I should probably have thrown myself on to it like a Hindu widow. But I didn't have nearly enough balls or strength of character to do that. Instead, I rented a lock-up garage a mile or so from where I lived, and I loaded the archive into its cardboard boxes, hired the white van, and began the removal process.

The garage was dry though not clean. It was windowless and no air circulated. It smelt of engine oil and there were bundles of old rags on the floor. I swept and cleaned up as best I could, but I couldn't rid the place, or myself, of an oppressive feeling of misery. The corrugated iron walls and roof were reminiscent of shanty towns, of pig pens and chicken coops. I didn't want to put my precious archive there, but what choice did I have?

It was hard work doing the job alone, but there was no possibility of getting help. The boxes of shoes were light enough, but the files and cuttings were heavy, and it was all imbued with a psychological as well as a physical weight. I was packing up a part of my own personality. In denying the archive I was also denying myself, and it occurred to me that these fetish objects which previously might have

183

been thought to be emblematic, indeed synecdochal, standing in as a substitute for a real woman or real sex, now seemed to be standing in as a substitute for me.

I made a half-hearted attempt to label the boxes but it was clearly pointless. Once they were in the garage, stacked on top of one another, few would be accessible, and in any case, I couldn't see myself needing access at the moment. Things had got too serious, too threatening, for me to want to toy with women's shoes, to want to pore over images of feet every evening.

Eventually my cellar was empty and the garage was full. I hooked a huge padlock on to the garage door and snapped it shut. The place looked reasonably secure but I could have wished for more. I needed a vault, a secret room, a cave guarded by mythical hounds. But this was going to have to do. Assuming there were no more developments and no revelations, no more visits from Crawford or his colleagues, then maybe a couple of months would be long enough to make me feel secure again. After that I could reclaim my archive, make it part of me again, return myself to myself. I looked forward hopefully to that day, but it never arrived.

Twenty-six

In the middle of all this madness Natasha arrived at my house. I hadn't given much thought to Mike and his problems recently, and even less to the reciprocal problems those were likely to have caused Natasha. I thought it was forgivable of me, granted the number of other things I had to worry about.

I'm sure it wasn't the first time I'd been alone with Natasha but I was used to functioning with her as part of a trio. She said she just happened to be in the area, which sounded very unconvincing, and I assumed she had come because I was a good friend and she wanted to talk about her and Mike. Again it seemed to confirm that I couldn't be a complete weirdo, not if people wanted to seek out my advice on their relationships. Not that I felt in any condition to give anybody advice on anything.

I tried to make Natasha welcome but I was relieved when she said she couldn't stay long. I offered her coffee and she said she could murder a drink, a real drink. So I gave her a gin and tonic. I had no way of knowing what Mike had said to her about his exploits in Birmingham and his desire to repeat them daily, so I wanted to wait for Natasha to bring up the subject. We talked breezily about nothing at all for fifteen minutes or so and then she said, 'Mike's told me all about you.'

That wasn't what I was expecting at all. I was lost for a reply.

'About your foot and shoe fetishism,' she added.

I could hardly be surprised that Mike had told her, but I couldn't see why she wanted to bring it up now.

'I don't think he approved,' I said. 'He thought it was rather pathetic of me.'

'He's a bit of a prude really, you know,' Natasha said.

There was no doubt some truth in that. I could see that the desire to do 'dirty' things with prostitutes could well stem from a puritanical frame of mind. Yet I didn't think that was really what Natasha meant. It seemed probable that Mike had told her all about me, but told her nothing at all about himself.

'It's no big deal,' I said. 'It's just a personal preference. It's just something I'm into, like some people are into mountaineering or motorcycle racing.'

This was idiotic nonsense but I hoped it would keep Natasha's interest at bay. This was not a moment when I wanted to explain and justify myself again. It didn't work.

'I think it's fascinating,' she said. 'I don't think it's pathetic at all.'

'Well, neither do I,' I said, then desperately changing the subject, 'And how is Mike?'

'How was he the last time you saw him?' she countered.

'A little the worse for wear,' I said. 'But it was a while ago.'

'Yes,' she agreed, though it wasn't at all clear what she was thinking about or what she was agreeing to.

Suddenly I found myself saying, 'I gather you and Mike are having a bad patch.'

I didn't know why I'd said it. It wasn't that I was eager to play therapist, or even that I was particularly interested.

'Something like that,' Natasha answered. 'I don't really want to talk about it. OK?'

'Fine,' I said. 'Fine.' But in that case, I wondered, what she *did* want to talk about, why she was paying me this visit. I soon found out. She kicked off her shoes, low-heeled, round-toed, black court shoes – nothing special – and revealed her bare feet. I've said before that Natasha's feet were pleasant enough, though not especially attractive to a man like myself. Now, however, she'd painted her nails a startling, uncharacteristic red, and while that didn't make the feet suddenly, overwhelmingly more appealing, it certainly caught the eye.

'Is that the kind of thing you like?' she asked.

I looked at her feet politely and said, 'Yes, that kind of thing.'

'What would you do with them?'

'Please,' I said. 'This is embarrassing.'

'Would you fondle them, stroke them, kiss them, slobber over them?'

'I suppose so, yes.'

'Would you like to do that now? To my feet?'

I was going to say something about Mike, about loyalty and friendship but Natasha stopped me and said, 'And if you remind me that I'm married to your best friend, I'll scream.'

'Don't scream,' I said.

She was sitting in a chair and I was sitting vulnerably on the sofa. She came to sit beside me. She positioned herself at the opposite end of the sofa so that her feet were resting in my lap. At first I did nothing, but the absurdity of sitting there inertly like that, like the reluctant, sexually timid hero of some kind of *Carry On* movie, got the better of me.

I started to stroke Natasha's feet. It was more of a massage than any version of foreplay, but Natasha seemed to be enjoying it a lot. She smiled and closed her eyes and threw her head back on to the arm of the sofa. As she did so her skirt rode up. I saw a long stretch of tanned thigh and I could see she was naked underneath the skirt. A dark, unruly pubic bush was clearly visible.

Now, I suppose if I had been a fetishist as per the classic case histories, Natasha's bare feet should have made me as horny as a polecat, while the pubic bush should have left me completely cold. But, in fact, given that I didn't find Natasha's feet all that erotic in the first place, the situation was reversed. While Natasha was becoming intensely aroused by having her feet stroked, I was becoming intensely aroused by the sight, presence and prospect of her bare cunt. And, after a while, after some deliberation and some amount of thinking about Mike, and after experiencing a certain, though highly equivocal, pang of guilt, I ran my hand all the way up Natasha's thigh. And then she *did* scream.

It wasn't one of those piercing, blood-curdling, ripper movie type screams that would bring neighbours running to lynch me, but it was an effective scream nevertheless. I immediately took my hands off her as though she was radioactive, I covered her legs with the flap of her skirt, and she leapt up off the sofa and ran across the room to get as far away from me as possible.

'This was a big mistake,' she said, more to herself than to me.

'I'm sorry,' I said.

'Yes,' she said again, just as inscrutably.

'I've not been myself lately,' I said.

'It's not your fault. It's my fault. And Mike's fault. He says I'm frigid. I think he's wrong.'

'Yes?' Now it was my turn to be inscrutable.

She stamped her feet into her shoes, thanked me for something or other, and she was gone.

Twenty-seven

I started to have dreams about Catherine; nightmares I suppose. They would always start out well enough. Catherine would have returned. There would be a chance meeting, a conversation, some hand-holding and kissing, and then a reconciliation. We would both say that we'd made mistakes and that we wanted to try again. Even in the dreams I was aware of the essential mawkish banality of this stuff but my subconscious was refusing to be serious and unsentimental. Then we would go to some anonymous dream room and Catherine would kick off her shoes and that's when all the problems would start.

In the least distressing of the dreams, the feet that were revealed were simply not Catherine's; they were not grotesque or deformed, not the genuine stuff of nightmares, but they just happened to be somebody else's. It was as though my whole reason for loving Catherine had been obliterated. It was terrible but not horrible. However, in another version of the dream I would discover that, at Kramer's suggestion, Catherine had had her feet tattooed with Harold's trade mark of footprint and lightning flash. The tattooing was garish and incompetent, done by some drug-stoked, cack-handed Hell's Angel. It was a form of sacrilege, of desecration, and even in the dream I was wondering whether laser technology and skin grafts could be used to return the feet to their natural state. It seemed to me that they couldn't, that the feet had been permanently damaged. Catherine, meanwhile, could never see what all the fuss was about.

And then came the worst dreams of all, the real stuff of a sick id on the rampage. In these Catherine would quite calmly tell me that she had developed a couple of open sores, one on each foot. But when she showed them to me it was obvious that these 'sores' were man-made, that someone (obviously Kramer) had driven nails into them, as if she had been nailed to a cross. I would run around looking for bandages, sticking plasters, TCP, Savlon; but the first-aid kit was always empty, the shops were always closed, there was nothing to be done, at which point Catherine would beg me to 'kiss them better'. I would try very hard, very desperately, but I could never quite force my lips to make contact with the pierced, bloody flesh.

My nights were getting tattered and sleepless, and to make matters worse Crawford took to ringing me in the early hours of the morning. The first time it happened I thought there must be some crisis, some dramatic development, but he simply asked me what kind of car I drove, and after I'd told him he put the phone down. The next time it was to ask whether I'd heard from Catherine; another time he simply said he'd been mulling over the case and wondered if I'd thought of anything new to tell him. It must have happened half a dozen times in all and there was never any point to it. It became obvious that he was doing it just to harass me. I thought he was trying to scare me, to wear me down, and he was succeeding.

And then a moment came when it seemed as if my waking life was taking on the same lurid, absurd texture as my dreams. I was hurrying to work in the rain, I was late, I'd been late a lot recently, and I noticed a chemist's window display and thought I must finally have snapped. There, blown up to a size that filled the whole of the window, was a giant black and white photograph of Catherine's naked feet. I stopped dead. I couldn't believe it. I would have preferred it to be a dream or hallucination. It seemed as though I might have gone completely mad and started to project images from my sick mind on to the world at large. And yet this particular image looked perfectly real and substantial. What's more, when I could think at all straight, I recognized that this was one of Kramer's photographs from the series I'd discovered in his studio. The bastard was dead but his art was living on. And once I'd managed to convince myself that the photograph did indeed exist in the real world, I soon realized this was *commercial* art. The words 'Adiol Footcare' had been superimposed in red lettering in the bottom right hand corner of the photograph. What I was looking at was a piece of advertising. Catherine's perfect, adored feet were being used to shift beauty products. Arranged in front of the giant blow up was an elaborate display of boxes, jars, tubes and sprays, all with the name Adiol on them.

I stood for a long time in front of that window. In other circumstances I might have been worshipping an erotic icon, but this time all I felt was bafflement and anger. At last I tore myself away and went into the shop. There I found an in-store display, a point-of-sale carousel, a pile of leaflets promoting the benefits of Adiol Footcare; and they all showed the same image of Catherine's feet.

I picked up a leaflet and opened it. It was full of stuff about how abused and neglected most people's feet are, and how they could become things of beauty if only you used Adiol footbaths, moisturizers, deodorants and so on. This sounded like complete guff to me. Catherine's feet, as

191

far as I knew, were a wonder of nature and, apart from her one visit to a pedicurist with me, owed nothing to Adiol or any other manufactured product.

After I'd been standing by the in-store display for a good few minutes a woman approached me. She wanted to sell me something. I could tell because she was wearing a yellow uniform with the Adiol logo printed on her left breast, and she asked me did I know that the average person takes eighteen thousand steps every day. I said I did, as a matter of fact, and that surprised her, so she simply asked me if I needed any help. I most certainly did, but not the kind she was likely to give me. All I said was, could she tell me where I might get hold of a copy of the poster. She was gently amused and said I was the third person to have asked her that and the display had only been up for an hour. She said the company didn't have any to give away, but maybe I could approach the photographer direct.

I lurched out into the street, picking up a fistful of leaflets as I went. So Kramer was an even more slimy piece of work than I'd imagined. At least my obsession with feet was personal, heartfelt and unexploitative. Kramer, it seemed, had wanted to make money out of his. Catherine really knew how to pick them. How could she let herself be used like that? For the very first time I thought that maybe Harold had done the right thing by killing Kramer.

Over the next week or two Catherine's feet appeared in shops and windows all over town. A walk down any street could become a journey of tantalizingly exquisite torture for me. Ads using the same image appeared in newspapers and magazines, even on bus stops. Catherine's feet must have found their way into hundreds of thousands, maybe even millions, of homes and psyches. Any common or garden foot fetishist or partialist could possess an image of

Catherine's feet. He could cut out the picture, put it in his scrapbook, his files, his archive. He could gloat and salivate and masturbate all over it. The idea made me simultaneously very angry and very horny. I wasn't pleased with myself for feeling like that. But what could I do? Catherine had always had a life of her own. Now the object of my private fascination was well and truly in the public domain.

Twenty-eight

I decided to return to Kramer's studio. This time I didn't intend to break in and I didn't intend to steal or destroy anything, but I did hope to get something I needed. I'd seen the reception area and the secretary's desk when I'd been there before. They suggested that Kramer's business wasn't entirely a one-man operation. I had reason to believe that it had enough momentum to keep going for a little while after his death, especially since examples of his work were currently on display everywhere. It was a long shot but I thought it was my only hope.

I went there in working hours, pressed the doorbell and hoped for the best. A woman's voice spoke in the entryphone and I muttered a few deliberately incomprehensible words. She said something equally incomprehensible in reply and pressed the buzzer that let me in.

I went up the stairs to the top of the building, to the studio, where I found a young woman in jeans and a lumberjack shirt, hair held back in a ponytail. She had her feet up on the desk and was smoking a joint. The place was a mess. There were boxes and tea chests all around her and it appeared she'd been half-heartedly packing and sorting through them. My presence gave her a surprise, and not a particularly pleasant one.

'Oh,' she said, 'I thought you were a messenger.'

'I'm a potential customer,' I said.

She looked confused.

'I'd like to see Mr Kramer,' I said brightly.

Then she appeared terribly sad. She wouldn't look me in the eye, and she said, 'He's passed away. I mean, he's dead. Robert's dead.'

'Dead?' I said. 'That's terrible. That's really terrible. I had no idea.'

'I'm just here holding the fort,' she said. 'Tidying up some loose ends. Sending out invoices. Paying bills.'

'But I keep seeing his work everywhere. The Adiol campaign.'

'Me too,' she said. 'It was all set up before he died, there was no reason to stop it. It breaks my heart every time I see it.'

'That must be awful for you.'

'It's not so great.'

'I'm so sorry,' I said. 'I really am. I'll go away and leave you to your work.'

I made as though to leave, but she said, 'Since you're here, what is it you wanted? Can I help?'

'It sounds trivial now,' I said. 'I wanted Mr Kramer to take some photographs for me, that's all. You see, I'm a shoe designer. I was so impressed by the photographs in the Adiol campaign I thought I'd like something similar to show off my own work.'

She didn't look at all perturbed. This was probably how things were done in her business; one job led to another, work generated work.

'It's a real shame,' she said. 'I'm sure he'd have been very interested. What can I say?'

'I'd better go,' I said.

'Hold on,' and she started looking through a fat address

book. 'I can give you the names of a couple of photographers who might be good for the job.'

'That's really kind of you,' I said.

She jotted down the names and phone numbers for me and handed over a slip of paper. 'They were both good friends of Robert's. He'd have been happy for them to have the work.'

She was sad again. She stared down at the address book and seemed hypnotized by it.

'It's a while since he died,' she said. 'I feel I ought to be getting over it by now.'

'It takes a lot of time,' I said. 'It takes as long as it takes.'

She nodded and looked at me as though I'd said something profound. I said goodbye and again started to leave.

'Oh, just one more thing,' I said. 'The model. You don't happen to know whose feet those are in the Adiol photographs?'

'Sure. She's not with an agency. But I can give you her name and phone number if you like.'

Casually, helpfully, undramatically, she wrote out Catherine's new phone number for me.

Twenty-nine

The number was not an American one after all. Catherine was still in the country somewhere. I looked in the book of dialling codes and saw it was in Yorkshire. I had no idea what she would be doing there. I hurried home and called the number. She answered the phone and her voice sounded so familiar, so untroubled, so far away from all the panic and fear I was going through.

'Hallo?' she said.

'Hallo, it's me.'

The effect was immediate. Her voice turned cold and hostile. 'How did you get this number?'

'It doesn't matter,' I said. 'What are you doing in Yorkshire?'

'Getting away from you. You shouldn't have called me.'

'I had to. I need you. I need your help. The police are after me. They seem to think I killed Kramer.'

She fell silent. I could feel aggression crackling down the phone at me. At last she said, 'Didn't you?'

'Are you crazy?' I said.

'Are you?'

I was in no state to make great claims for my sanity and rationality, but it had never occurred to me that Catherine might think I was a murderer.

'If you really think I did it then why haven't you been to the police?' I said.

'Because I'm a fool. Because I don't want you to go to prison, I guess. And that's because I guess I'm still in love with you.'

That was a real shock.

'I never knew you were in love with me at all,' I said.

'It took me a while to realize.'

'You've picked a great moment to tell me. Why did you go off with Kramer?'

'I didn't go off with him. I fucked him once or twice, that's all. It started out as a professional relationship, as a matter of fact. And it was mostly your fault.'

'Hey!' I protested. 'Come on.'

'It's true,' she insisted. 'You made me realize I had a pair of pretty special feet. I thought others might think so too. I talked to a few people and they put me in touch with Kramer, this guy who needed a foot model for a campaign he was shooting. That's all. That's how it started. And it would have ended just as quickly. He was a sleaze. But you shouldn't have followed us. You shouldn't have been waiting in the car. That made me mad. And you shouldn't have killed him.'

'I didn't.'

'So who did?'

'Harold', I said.

'Harold? Oh, get real. Harold couldn't kill anybody.'

'But you think I could?'

'Oh shit, I don't know.'

I did my best to explain what little I understood about Harold's state of mind, and what I imagined to be his motives for killing Kramer.

'That's terrible, if it's true,' she said. 'Poor Harold. So why don't *you* go to the police?'

'Because I think they won't believe me. Why would they

if you don't? But all this is beside the point. I want to see you. Can I see you?'

'No, not yet. Maybe not ever. I don't know. Why? What would we do?'

'Talk about the good old days?' I suggested.

'I'm going to have to think about all this,' she said. 'I don't know. Jesus. I don't know what to believe.'

Later that night she rang me back. It felt like an enormous breakthrough, a great concession on her part, and she sounded much softer, much more sympathetic.

'Look,' she said. 'Have I got this right? There's nothing that connects you to the murder. No hard evidence. Is that so?'

'Nothing directly,' I said. 'But there's plenty of circumstantial.'

I thought about my archive, about that dirty corrugated-iron garage and I wished I could somehow magically make it disappear.

'In the absence of real evidence they'd never convict you, right?' Catherine said.

'Your faith in British justice is touching,' I said.

'Let me finish. But there's even less evidence to connect the murder to Harold. You could say he did it, he could say you did it. Stalemate. That could happen, couldn't it?'

'I suppose.'

'One or other of you would have to confess.'

'What do you mean, one or other of us? I have nothing to confess to. Do you still not believe me?'

'I want to believe you. I think I do, but I need to do something first.'

She wouldn't tell me what that something was. She put down the phone. My brain felt as though it was about to caramelize and I decided I was going to destroy my archive.

Thirty

When I got to the row of lock-ups I could see there was a man hanging around, more or less where my own garage was, and it took me longer than it should have to realize that the man was Crawford. I was tempted to turn and run, but it was obvious that Crawford had seen me even before I saw him, and he would no doubt have given chase. More importantly, if he was hanging around near the archive I wanted to be there too, to protect it if nothing else, although that seemed pretty absurd given that I'd gone there to destroy it.

I kept walking towards Crawford and he watched me, but his face showed no more emotion than if he had been staring at a blank television screen. Even when I got to the door of the garage he didn't say anything, just stepped back and gestured that I should go ahead and unlock the door. He watched as I turned the key in the padlock and his scrutiny made me clumsy, but at last I fumbled the door open and swung it aside, and I looked into the garage to see that it was completely empty. It had been cleaned out, swept bare so that it ached with absence. I turned to Crawford and at last he was animated.

'I just wanted to see your face when you opened that garage,' he said, and he chuckled and looked nauseatingly pleased with himself.

'What's going on?' I asked.

'I've borrowed your little collection, OK?'

'No, it's not OK.'

'Tough.'

'What do you want?'

'I want a bit of co-operation. I want you to help me with my inquiries. The usual stuff. You don't mind, do you? Well, it's all the same if you do. Now, I could take you down the station, do it all properly, get you to make a statement, offer you a legal representative, that kind of crap, but I think it'd be better if we kept it nice and casual, don't you?'

I certainly didn't want to be formally questioned in some police station, but there was something about Crawford's use of the world casual that promised the worst. I didn't know what to say or do, but it soon became obvious that nothing I said or did was going to make any difference. A white car appeared out of nowhere and Crawford bundled me into the back of it. The car was unmarked but it had a police radio and there was a young, gaunt, red-haired man driving.

'This is Angus,' Crawford said, giving no indication whether that was the driver's first or second name. 'He's a gem.'

I saw that the dashboard was littered with chewing-gum wrappers, and the interior of the car smelt of spearmint and Kentucky fried chicken. Angus drove fast and angrily. He was in a terrible hurry to get me where I was going.

'Am I under arrest?' I asked.

'Oh, grow up,' Crawford said, and the driver laughed.

I didn't say anything after that, just looked out of the window until our destination came into sight; a small industrial building that might once have been a factory or warehouse. Now it looked unused and abandoned, but a sliding door was open in the side wall and there was an empty police van parked beside it. Angus stopped the car and the three of us went into the building. I wondered if I was about to experience some much-mythologized police brutality.

There were no windows in the walls of the building, but the roof had glass panels, and light fanned down to the floor beneath to where my entire archive was immaculately, systematically, and above all, nakedly, laid out. The books and files had been subdivided into orderly piles, and all the hundreds of shoes were laid out in pairs, in neatly engineered rows. I had never seen my archive from this perspective. It was like looking down on a futuristic city with its thoroughfares and high-rises. I felt strangely moved. Two uniformed policemen were moving among the rows, noting things down in notebooks, attempting to categorize and catalogue what they saw. They looked up as the three of us came in. They shrugged and laughed, to show that they thought this work was absurd and beneath their dignity. Nevertheless, they were treating the archive with a touching degree of care.

We walked through the building until we came to a small, partitioned office. It had windows of wired glass but newspaper had been stuck over them to prevent anyone seeing in. There were three chairs in the office, made of an inappropriately cheerful orange plastic. Crawford had me sit down in the middle chair, slammed the office door shut and said, 'OK, now all you have to do is tell me everything.'

Some hours later I was tired, confused, scared and no longer sure of what I was saying or of what I knew. I had indeed tried to tell them 'everything'; all about me and my fetishism, about Catherine and Harold and Kramer. All about Alicia and the man from the ICA. I'd explained my archive,

202

the reason for its existence, the way it had been created. I'd even told them about Natasha, in the forlorn hope that would make me seem more 'normal'. The only thing I'd kept back, and I was quite proud of myself for doing it, was the fact that I'd spoken to Catherine and knew her phone number.

Not that it made any difference. Crawford didn't seem to believe much of what I said, and what he did believe he didn't like. His colleague had said barely three words during the whole session, but he didn't have to speak. He was there to ooze menace and anger and contempt, and he was good at it. He was a natural. But eventually a moment came when I had no more to say, nothing else to reveal about myself. I fell into a profound, enervated silence, at which point Crawford perked up.

'Right then, let's see how much wiser I am than when we started. We've established that you like feet and shoes. You like them so much you're prepared to harass women in the street over them. You're prepared to make a criminal of yourself by stealing them. You put together a sick little "archive", and you go to clubs that celebrate "sexual difference", and you go to prostitutes and you beat up men that you've picked up at the ICA.

'Now, we don't know why you're this way. It could be your mother's fault for not giving you enough tit when you were a kid, or it could be because you were once scared by a bare fanny. But either way it doesn't make any difference, does it, because you say you're very happy to live with this fetish of yours.'

I nodded. For a moment I thought he was being sympathetic.

'Now,' he continued, 'as far as I can see, this means that when you get a bird in the bedroom it doesn't matter what

203

her face is like, what her figure's like, all you're interested in is her plates of meat. And when she lets you have your way, you make straight for the tootsies. You like to snog 'em, drool over 'em, wank over 'em. Have I got all this right?'

It wasn't only his choice of vocabulary that vulgarized and misrepresented me. The mere fact of being described by Crawford was belittling in itself. Nevertheless I nodded, didn't argue, agreed to his crass, cartoon version of myself.

'So, anyway,' Crawford continued, 'you find this Catherine, this perfect woman with this perfect pair of feet, and she lets you do all this weird stuff to her and you like that a lot, a helluva lot. You think this must be the Real Thing. The pervert's suddenly in love. But then she leaves you for this geezer Kramer, who also appears to like a good pair of feet and who happens to get murdered not long after. Funny old world, isn't it?

'However, by now we've switched into fairy-tale mode, haven't we? Now we get the quaint old shoemaker who makes fabulous fuck-me shoes and does a little bit of murder and mutilation on his day off. And wouldn't you know it, the bugger's now gone and disappeared. Am I still on the right track, here? I haven't lost the plot yet, have I?'

'No,' I said.

Crawford turned away from me and addressed his next remarks to his colleague.

'I don't know what you think, Angus, but I don't think we need all this crud about fetishism. It's highly colourful as a bit of motivation, but I don't see that it's necessary at all. I don't see that we need Freud or Krafft-bloody-Ebing or even the old shoemaker. Some bloke steals your bird so you kill him. Sounds a bit drastic but it's perfectly straightforward, happens every day, doesn't it?'

Angus nodded but still said nothing.

'Kramer was a very nasty piece of work,' Crawford said to me. 'We know that. Photography was the least of what he was into. Nasty stuff. I'd rather not go into details. Personally I wouldn't blame you at all for killing him.'

He gave a fake sympathetic smile.

'But the mutilation, that was going a bit far, wasn't it? Don't you think?'

'I don't know anything about the mutilation,' I said.

'Take your shirt off,' Crawford instructed.

I hesitated for a moment and that was too long for him. He grabbed the front of my shirt and ripped it open. He took a black felt-tip pen and began to draw on my chest. I looked down, unable at first to decipher the drawing but I soon realized that he'd drawn a crude version of Harold Wilmer's trade mark: the footprint and the lightning flash.

'That's what you did to Kramer, isn't it?' said Crawford. 'Except you used a knife instead of a pen.'

I shook my head in denial and disbelief.

'Is that really what he did?' I asked.

'It's what *you* did,' he said. 'But, then, you probably know people who do that kind of thing for kicks.'

It didn't seem to matter what I said any more. I was long past lying or trying to please my interrogator. I looked Crawford in the eye and said, 'If you really think I'm capable of murdering a man and slashing designs on his chest with a knife, then you're even more stupid than I thought you were.'

I was ready for him to turn nasty but in fact he appeared to be amused.

'You're good, I'll give you that,' he said. 'I mean, you're very convincing. It would be easy to believe you didn't do it. What do you think, Angus?'

Crawford's colleague looked at me dispassionately, apparently disinterestedly, and said, 'I think he did it.'

'You could be right,' Crawford said. Then he became very thoughtful and said to me, 'Right, I want to try out a little theory of mine. Get on the floor, on your hands and knees.'

I hesitated again, but not for long. Crawford pulled me off my chair and threw me on the ground. I got into a kneeling position. There was a horrible inevitability about what happened next as Crawford kicked off his right shoe, a highly polished black Oxford, pulled off his nylon sock and shoved his bare foot into my face.

'Suck it,' he said. 'Suck it the way you'd suck Catherine's.'

'No,' I said.

Crawford barely reacted. He still didn't look angry, but he tilted his head towards his colleague who immediately got up and kicked me at the base of my spine. The effect was truly staggering, as though my back had been turned into a piano keyboard, and every key was playing a separate note of pain.

'We can try that game too,' said Crawford. 'But you'll lose and you'll still have to suck it.'

So I sucked the bastard's foot. Why not? It was loathsome and filthy, it tasted of bad meat, of rubber and decaying metal. The nails were sharp and horny, the toes bristling with black hairs. The flesh was soft and damp with sweat. But what did it matter? I sucked it, not quite the way I'd have sucked Catherine's, but not so very differently. It occurred to me then that these two men might do anything to me; beat me, fuck me, kill me. Anything. But Crawford suddenly withdrew his foot from my mouth.

'No, sorry, Tiger,' he said. 'Doesn't do a thing for me. Seems I'm not a pervert after all.'

He was putting his shoe and sock back on when there

was a knock on the door and one of the uniformed policemen put his head round to tell Crawford he was wanted on the phone. He left the office and I was left with Angus. In Crawford's absence he relaxed a lot, became a lot less angry. He offered me a cigarette, but I turned it down.

'Very sensible,' he said. Then, obviously thinking of Crawford, he continued, 'He's a cunt, but he's good.'

Crawford returned a minute later. Now his face looked bruised with a hot flush of blood. He was in a rage, his hands were trembling.

'I wonder if you could leave us alone now, Angus?' he said, his voice straining to stay in control.

Angus looked very surprised.

'You were wrong,' Crawford said to him. 'He didn't do it.'

Angus left the office. Crawford slammed the door after him and I felt extremely frightened.

'We had a phone call,' Crawford said. 'You didn't do it.'

'What phone call?' I said. 'Who from?'

Ignoring my questions he said, 'I'm very sorry you didn't do it, actually. I wish you had. But it seems you're not a murderer after all, just a toe-rag.' He laughed heartily to himself, then added, 'I've been waiting a long time to say that. Get up.'

He led me out of the office into the main body of the building where my archive was still all laid out. There was nobody there now. The uniformed police had gone, and through the open doors I could see that Angus was waiting behind the wheel of the white car.

'This little collection of yours is the most pitiful thing I've seen in years,' said Crawford. 'It's fucking sad. You turn my stomach, you know that? But you didn't kill Kramer.'

'Of course I didn't,' I said.

'And you didn't carve a footprint on his chest, among other things.'

'I know,' I said.

Crawford hit me a number of times; in the face, in the balls, and in the stomach and kidneys after I'd fallen to the ground. None of them hurt nearly as much as the single blow from his colleague had, but he seemed to be satisfied with what he'd done. He walked away, out of the building to the waiting car. I heard the door slam and the car pull away long before I was able to stand and walk.

When I eventually gathered my wits together, I sat up and looked at the archive arranged around me. It was unharmed and intact. It wouldn't have been so hard to gather it together as best I could, hire another van maybe, take it all home with me, return it to my cellar. Nothing physical had been destroyed, nothing should have changed, and yet, having been exposed to scrutiny and scorn, the objects in the archive had lost their magic. The fetishes had been stripped of their power. I didn't need them any more. I had no further use for them. I stood up painfully and limped away from it all.

Thirty-one

The most important scene in this whole drama took place in my absence. I wasn't there. I didn't see what happened or how or why, and the two people who *were* there have very good reasons for refusing to tell me the precise details.

First, what I *do* know. It appears that Harold Wilmer's disappearance was not as complete as I had imagined. Although he abandoned his shop and made himself unavailable both to me and to the police, he never lost touch with Catherine. In fact I discovered that even before then, Catherine and Harold had been in regular contact. I know now that they continued to see each other after Catherine and I split up. I know now that he continued to make shoes for her. I also know that she never told him she was seeing Kramer, and when he found out, when I told him, that's when he decided to become a murderer. And once Kramer was dead he broke the news to Catherine, only he told her I was the one who'd done it.

After I tracked down Catherine and spoke to her on the phone, when I put the idea in her mind that perhaps I wasn't the murderer after all, that Harold was, she knew exactly how to find him and she did so. Catherine is no fool. She put two and two together and realized that I was likely to be telling the truth, that Harold might indeed have killed Kramer, and subsequently she managed to convince Harold to turn himself in and make a full confession. She took him along to the police where he told them everything, much more than I could have. They believed him, and shortly thereafter someone made a phone call to Crawford, and that was the only reason he decided that I hadn't committed the murder.

Those are the bare bones of the story, and I have probably spent too much time trying to put flesh on them. I realized it was unreasonable of me but I was angry and upset to learn that Catherine and Harold had seen each other in my absence. I felt betrayed. I thought they had no connection except through me, and I wanted it to remain that way. I picture them in Harold's workshop, or later in some secret unknown place, Catherine arriving, Harold proffering the latest pair of shoes. I can see his leathery old hands slipping some flimsy, exotic creation on to Catherine's perfect foot. I see her walking across the room, turning, posing, wheeling on tiptoe. I know that all this must have really happened.

Of course, I see a powerful erotic element here, and sometimes my vision of the scene takes on a pornographic, fantastical aspect. Then I visualize Catherine being naked, except for the shoes, displaying herself, showing herself to Harold. Sometimes his involvement is simply voyeuristic, he simply watches and is appreciative. But other times he touches, strokes, kisses, penetrates. And she reciprocates, runs her hands, lips, feet, over Harold's old, small, sagging body.

I don't know if that really happened or not. Catherine won't tell me and perhaps I should be grateful not to know, but there are times when it seems all too likely. For Catherine it would have been just another adventure, and if Harold really was sexually involved with her that would give him much more reason for killing Kramer.

And I wonder sometimes how Catherine got him to confess to the murder. I have asked her, and she tells me she appealed to his better nature, but I know that's just an evasive joke. I can easily envisage a number of perverse scenarios; the two of them together, naked, in bed, or on the floor, or in a hotel, or out of doors, Catherine in tortuously high heels egging him on, apparently for some sort of weird sexual gratification. 'Did you ever kill a man, Harold? Did you strip him naked? Did you mutilate the body? Did you carve your trade mark in his chest?' And Harold says yes, he did, he did all that and more, and he did it for her because he was in love with her. And perhaps Catherine is filled with horror and immediately disentangles herself from his embrace, but it seems equally likely that she'd wait until he'd finished, until the old bones and the old flesh had concluded their business. And then she tells him the game is up, that she knows everything, that she'll blow the whistle if he doesn't turn himself in.

Or perhaps none of that happened at all, perhaps he was simply so besotted with Catherine, so in thrall to her, that all she needed to do was tell him to confess and he would immediately obey.

But even as these thoughts first occurred to me, I knew that in one sense none of it really mattered. I didn't enjoy thinking of Catherine with Harold, but I knew that for her it was just another sexual adventure, quite a colourful one, managing to sleep with the fetishist and the creator of the fetish objects, with the murderer and the victim, but it was no *more* than an adventure. It was not love.

Besides, how could I feel resentful towards her? She saved me in more ways than one. I owed her everything. I knew I was still in love with her, and the weird thing was, I was no longer only in love with her feet.

Thirty-two

It is 1966 in California and a group of young male student volunteers are sitting in a darkened lecture theatre on a distant part of the campus waiting for the slide show to begin. They have all stated that they are heterosexuals and that they are not foot or shoe fetishists. They have signed the appropriate forms, received a small cash payment, and they sit in their seats, their genitals wired up to electrical devices that measure the degree of their sexual arousal.

The projector kicks into life and the first slide appears; a picture of a woman's high-heeled shoe. Then a slide of a slingback, then of a patent leather thigh boot. This goes on for some time. The guys giggle and get restless. Is this really what they've been brought here for? Then things get better. A new set of slides appears; a naked woman, *Playboy*-style, big breasted, air-brushed, not the girl next door. More giggles now, but of a different sort; they start to enjoy themselves and the display of naked female flesh continues till the end of the session when the projector dies, and the lights are switched on again. No word of explanation is forthcoming from the research staff as they unhook the electrical devices and tell the boys to come back next week for more of the same.

Once they've gone, the psychologists running the experiment, Rachman and Hodgson as they are known in the literature, scrutinize each subject's arousal chart. They are as predicted: nothing when the shoes appear on the screen, but the moment the naked women appear there's lots of vigorous, boyish arousal. Well, thinks Rachman, that could be changed.

Time passes. The students attend the weekly sessions, and on each occasion it's the same procedure; sitting there wired up, looking at footwear followed by cheesecake. A few of the guys have started to find this whole thing totally ridiculous. There are strange things happening on every campus in America but this feels stranger than most. Still, the process isn't arduous, it seems perfectly harmless and the money is worth having. Besides, the number of sessions is finite. The last session soon arrives. The students go into the lecture theatre and are appropriately blasé as they get wired up and take their seats for a final session of the same old thing. But this time there's a surprise.

The room dims, the projector starts, and the slides of women's shoes duly appear. But that's all there is. This time the naked babes don't put in an appearance. The students watch a slide show that consists entirely of women's shoes. A couple of the guys make loud complaints but Rachman and Hodgson check the arousal meters and they see that five of the guys are every bit as aroused as they would be by watching slides of naked women. Five brand-new fetishists have been created. In some quarters this would be called a success.

I don't find this piece of research particularly reassuring. It seems to suggest that there's nothing very profound or deep-rooted about fetishism. Fetishists, it appears, can be created from scratch in no time at all. Fetishism, the experiment seems to imply, is just a form of conditioning, no more complex or crucial than being swayed by a TV commercial.

You see an ad on TV. It tells you that you need some new product. You never knew you needed it, but that's because you'd never been told that you did. Now that you've been told, you know that you want it. It has become an object of desire, separate from all the rest of the world of objects. It has become a fetish. You have become a fetish-ist. If it works with soap powders and cars and tampons, then why shouldn't it work with shoes and feet or any other damn thing? As I have said, I think we are all fetishists, but when I said it before I was only talking about sex and these days I think sex isn't even the half of it.

There is the world and there is the individual. The world is vast, complex and complete, and we as individuals are none of the above. We live in our small corners, trying to catch a glimpse of the ground plan, the overall structure, but we never quite do. We only get to see architectural details: the finials, the gargoyles. It never quite makes sense, and artists' impressions aren't much use in this area.

There are people who profess to have some notion of the grand design, who claim to understand whole systems; the true believers, the conspiracy theorists. But I think they're mistaken. Believing in the cross, or in the free market or in any other damn thing seems every bit as partial as 'believing in' women's feet or shoes. These systems themselves are still only synecdoches, relics, fetishes.

But I happen to think this isn't so terrible. We deal with what we can. We try to bite off no more than we can chew. We prefer to feel at home within the limits of our own space and our own understanding, rather than to be adrift and lost in the random world. We like the familiar.

You can't transform the world so you redecorate your

living room. You can't love the whole world so you do your best with your spouses, your lovers, your children, your parents, your pets.

What do we see as we walk down the street? It's not an egalitarian mass of light waves and ambient noise, it isn't just atoms and vibrations, all sensory data of equivalent value. In order to see it at all we create separations, reductions, groupings. The window cleaner walks down the street and sees only windows that need cleaning. The Peeping Tom sees openings into new worlds. The boy with a slingshot sees only targets.

Sure we're looking for wholeness, but where are you going to find it? We slice up the encyclopaedia into part works, manageable morsels, only what the reader can digest. Everybody selects, and the things we select might be called our interests, our obsessions, our fetishes. But they are more than that. These 'selections' are what constitute our lives.

One day Catherine came back. I was alone in my house. It was night. I was free, whatever that meant. Crawford was off my back and Harold was behind bars, although his trial was still a long way off. I was slumped in a chair drinking cheap lager and watching a hired video. I knew this looked pathetic, and it was not the way I would have wanted Catherine to find me, but then again I wasn't expecting to be found. The doorbell rang and I came close to not answering it. There was nobody I wanted to see, no arrival that I thought I would have welcomed. But for some reason I did answer the door and there she was, Catherine, looking somehow very different and somehow very much the same. The hair was a shade lighter, the skin had a tan, and she was wearing unfamiliar clothes, a version of western gear:

jeans and a denim jacket, an embroidered shirt, fancy cowboy boots.

'I'm not interrupting am I?' she asked as she slid past me into the house. 'Have you missed me?'

There was no point playing it cool.

'What do you think?' I said.

'You had the shoes,' she replied. 'Some photographs, the plaster casts. Wasn't that enough?'

'You know it wasn't.'

'Good,' she said. 'I missed you too.' Coming from Catherine that was quite a confession. 'I'm sorry,' she said. 'Sorry about various things. You don't need me to specify, do you?'

'I suppose not.'

'Poor old Harold,' she said.

Sympathy was only the slightest of a whole bundle of feelings I currently had towards Harold, but to be charitable I said, 'Yes, poor old Harold.'

She sat down, leaned back into a corner of the sofa and put her feet up on the opposite arm. She looked perfectly relaxed and at home.

'Are you back?' I asked uncertainly, not knowing exactly what I meant by 'back'.

'Well, I'm here,' she said.

'Are you staying?'

'Sure.'

'Do you want anything? A drink?'

'You could help me off with my boots.'

I've always quite liked cowboy boots as objects; their shape, their style, the way in which their essence always remains much the same and yet they're a canvas for all kinds of aesthetic transformations. But I had never found them erotic, and the ones Catherine was wearing – purple and black, very pointed and heavily stitched – were really no exception. However, what the boots contained was still a subject of utmost erotic fascination for me. That hadn't changed or diminished. I did indeed want to help her off with her boots so I could get at her feet. Mindful that some of my bad dreams might have been prophetic, I was ready for the worst as I pulled off the boots. I needn't have worried; there were no tattoos, no scars, no stigmata.

'I've been looking after them,' she said. 'Though probably not as well as you would have.'

I held her feet in my hands. They were perfect, of course, as pale and pure and cold as vellum. I kissed them, let my lips move softly and drily over their insteps. They were exactly as I remembered them.

'I've really missed that,' said Catherine, but she was only saying what I might have said. 'You've done a job on me,' she continued. 'You've turned me into a mirror-image of you. You want to worship feet. I want to have my feet worshipped. I guess we've turned into the perfect couple.'

So she moved in. And it was strange, very strange, but it was good. We had plenty of wild, intense, unorthodox, fetishistic sex, but we also had a surprising amount of wild, intense, orthodox, unfetishistic sex; sex in which feet and shoes hardly figured at all.

We didn't go to sex clubs, and when we were in wine bars I generally didn't take her shoes away and masturbate into them. And instead of bringing strange women round to participate in three-way sex we simply had people round for dinner. I got in touch with Mike and Natasha again, made no reference to the strange scenes I'd gone through with both of them. They were as keen to deny history as I was, and they were eager to meet Catherine. 'My God,' they said after they'd met her. 'Where have you been hiding

217

her? She's just what you've always needed.' I was glad they liked her, and they seemed genuinely pleased on my behalf, but I also knew they were relieved that I'd finally found someone. I think I was relieved too.

It was two o'clock on Sunday morning. Mike and Natasha had been round for dinner and had only just left. The room was a mess with dirty plates, empty glasses and wine bottles, and Catherine and I were both tired and comfortably drunk. In general we didn't spend much time talking about Harold or Kramer or the murder, but we didn't specifically avoid it either, didn't want to turn it into a taboo subject. However, if we wanted to talk about it at all, it was easiest when the night was old and we were nicely drunk.

This time Catherine said, 'You know Harold made shoes for me after I stopped seeing you?'

I did, of course.

'Well, want to see 'em?'

It would have been cowardly to say no, so, with a lot of trepidation and some of the old anticipation, I agreed. Catherine stepped out of the living room into the hallway and I could hear a rustling of boxes and tissue paper, then the sound of clothing being removed, and when Catherine returned she was naked except for a pair of shoes I'd never seen before.

They were surprisingly restrained for a pair of Harold's. The heels were very high and the toes were very pointed, but there was none of the baroque, erotic splendour that characterized so many of his shoes, nor did they appear to be made from any exotic fabric. They were elegant, classic, if slightly exaggerated, court shoes in a plain, rich brown leather. I was slightly disappointed.

Catherine pulled up a dining chair and sat in front of me,

218

opened her legs, raised them and placed one foot on each of my shoulders. I turned and kissed the tops of her feet and my eyes came very close to the shoes. The grain of the leather was strangely smooth and unmarked. It was less commonplace than I'd thought. It had a fine, waxy texture to it, and it was clearly not calf, not pigskin, not kid, in fact, not anything I'd ever seen before, at least not in this form.

And then I remembered what Crawford had said about Kramer's mutilation. He'd said that Harold's trade mark had been carved into the dead man's chest, but he'd added 'among other things'. I sniffed at the shoes, ran my fingers over them.

I said to Catherine, 'They could be made out of human skin, couldn't they?'

'Couldn't they just,' she said.